# *A Tempting Ruin*

by

Kristin Vayden

A Tempting Ruin
by Kristin Vayden
published by Blue Tulip Publishing
www.bluetulippublishing.com




ISBN 13: 978-1515244875
ISBN: 1515244873
Cover Art Designed by Melody Pond

*To my mom, who has faced life fearlessly.*
*God has completely brought you through every obstacle,*
*especially your recent fight against cancer.*
*And each day I'm thankful for your love, wisdom, insight,*
*and strength as you point me to Jesus, our Savior.*

*I love you, Momma,*
*and just because I know you're thinking it right now,*
*I love YOU more!*

# PROLOGUE

AT FIRST, SHE THOUGHT SHE WAS ALONE.

To be honest, at first she was… sitting in front of the fire in a rather comfortable chaise and immersing herself in a fantastic book.

Then the door opened and closed so quietly she almost didn't glance up from her page.

However, as providence would have it, she did indeed glance up and saw a gentleman enter and stride purposefully toward the window overlooking the back wood.

She should have spoken up, for it was forbidden to be in a room alone with an available gentleman, but she couldn't find the moral power to open her mouth. Rather, she simply watched him.

His olive-green jacket accentuated his shoulders, and the tan breeches highlighted the contour of his muscular legs.

He was glorious, with raven black hair cut shorter than the common style, but it fit his angular jawline, or what she could see of it. The rest she imagined, knowing his face, having seen him before, but it was unlikely that he could boast the same recognition of her.

"Are you quite done?" he asked, causing a painful blush to heat her face as she realized he was aware of her study of his person.

However, feeling a bit of her hoyden streak, she simply replied, "No, if you'll please shift to the side however…"

His slow turn as he shifted to face her gave a view of his amused expression as he held out his hands, proving his amicability to her request.

"Is this better?"

"Indeed. Though I must ask why you felt it necessary to hide in the library," Beatrix asked, setting her book aside and straightening her posture.

"I aim to please." He nodded then took a few lazy steps toward her. "I'm not hiding… I'm simply… enjoying some peace."

"In a room you thought to be empty?"

"What if I told you… I knew it wouldn't be empty."

"Then I'd say that I'm no fool… easily led to believe a lie," she shot back. "I have sisters, you know."

"Indeed… Miss Beatrix." He bowed then raised a daring eyebrow.

"Hmm… either we've been introduced, and I've already forgotten your person — which isn't a recommendation — or you're exceedingly forward."

"Says the lady that just asked me to turn for her visual benefit."

"True…" Beatrix shrugged. "…though I am curious how you know my name, Lord Neville."

"Ah, so I am not unknown. You are indeed a minx, are you not?" he teased.

Beatrix studied him. This was likely the oddest conversation she'd ever have in her life… completely against the rules of society. Yet it was entirely diverting!

"Perhaps."

"Ah, keep your secrets then." He shrugged and then

approached her, glancing at her book. "Enjoying it?"

"I was..." Beatrix let the words linger.

"You wound me. Is my sparkling conversation not enough to satisfy your need for amusement?"

"No." She shrugged and picked up her book. She studied the page for a moment while watching him from the corner of her eye.

His grin broke through, giving her an unfocused view of his white teeth.

"It's working, you know." He spoke as he moved to sit in the wingback chair across from her.

"What is working?" she asked dryly as she continued to study the page.

"Graham is practically going mad."

At this, Beatrix glanced up, feeling her brow furrow. "I'm sure I don't understand what you mean." How was it possible that he had caught on to their ploy? In truth, the whole house party was simply a strategy to get Lord Graham to finally offer for her sister; helped along by the implication that Lord Neville was pressing his suit for Bethanny's hand as well. Even if he wasn't...but *he* wasn't supposed to know it wasn't true! Either of them!

"Do not pretend with me. Anyone with half the sense of a toad can discern your stratagem. I was just letting you know it was indeed successful. I must admit that adding my involvement was a nice touch. Though I'd never actually offer for Miss Lamont, I could have put on quite the show." He shook his head.

"Who are you?" Beatrix felt the need to ask. How was it possible he knew so much about their private endeavors?

"Edwin Rowland, Eighth Earl of Neville, my lady." He gave a jaunty nod of his chin.

She studied him then tentatively offered her own name. "Beatrix Lamont, Miss Lamont to you."

"A lovely name, I say."

"Thank you."

The silence lingered for a few moments, but it wasn't uncomfortable, rather a peaceful lull.

Beatrix lifted her book once more.

"What is it you are reading?"

"Ah, I doubt you'd approve." She shot him a glance over the page.

"Try me."

*"Lady Maybelle's Mysterious Suitor."*

"It's the butler." He leaned forward and grinned evilly.

"What? No. You did not… I—" Beatrix stood, closed the book and paced irritatedly. Opening the book, she glanced to the last page and read, her fury rising by the moment.

"It *was* the butler! You ruined it!" she all but shouted as she lifted the book. For a fleeting moment, she wanted to throw it at him! How dare he ruin the fantastic book, the sweet mystery, by giving away the ending! Of all her pet peeves, this was champion.

"I do hope you're a poor aim if you decide to follow through with hurling the volume at my head." He stood and held up his hands.

"Why? Why would you *do* that?" Beatrix lamented, tossing the book on the chaise and glaring at him.

"Because it amuses me."

She stilled, knowing her glare grew more menacing by the moment as she studied the horrible creature she had, only moments ago, thought so devastatingly attractive. "It… amuses you?"

"Rather, *you* amuse me. Your reaction." He lifted his shoulder in a blasé manner, as if he hadn't just provoked her!

"I — you — you!" Beatrix ground out then stomped.

"Did you just stomp?" he asked, his grin growing.

"A lady doesn't stomp. There was a spider," she lied and stalked away toward the window, hoping the horrible man would get the point and take his leave.

The sound of footsteps approaching had her stiffening her back.

"I'm sorry for offending you so greatly. But I do thank you for being the cause of such a prized few moments of amusement. It was… delightful. And I'll tell you a secret…" His voice was close, sending prickles of awareness up her arms as his velvet voice spoke softly.

"Humbled to be your entertainment, sir," she replied frostily, trying to keep her reaction to him hidden away and forgotten. Turning to face him, she shifted her gaze from him to the door meaningfully.

His amused chuckle was the only response.

*Drat.*

"If you read the next book, you'll find out a little bit more about the butler… because, Miss Beatrix, things are not what they always seem," he replied kindly and then turned to leave.

"Wait," she called out before she thought about it.

He paused and turned to her, his grey eyes clear and completely drawing her in. "You don't have to leave just yet."

"I do believe that is the kindest thing you've said to me." He bit back a grin.

Barely resisting the urge to roll her eyes, Beatrix walked over to the bookshelf where she had originally found the book and looked for the sequel. "What is the title of the second book?" she called over her shoulder.

Lord Neville smiled and glanced down, then strode toward her. *"The Butler's Secret."*

"Oh! I can't wait." She smiled as she searched for the book. "Ah! There it is!" She stood on her very tiptoes, reaching for the book, her fingers brushing the spine and missing in the effort to withdraw it.

"Blast it all," she mumbled.

"Such language from a lady!" Lord Neville scolded, tsking his tongue.

In spite of his grin, which bespoke his unoffended nature,

Beatrix still felt her face heat with a painful blush.

"Allow me."

"No, I've got it." Beatrix tried again.

"Very well." Lord Neville stepped back, crossing his arms.

After several additional attempts to dislodge the book, Beatrix sighed and turned to face him. "Can you please help?"

"I thought you'd never ask, though I must say the… stretching… offered a very pleasant view of your ankles," he replied as he brushed past her and began to reach for the book.

"Ooo…" Beatrix elbowed him in the ribs just as he stretched.

"What the—" He dislodged the book only slightly and turned to glare at her. "Was that necessary?"

"You were looking at my ankles," she replied haughtily.

"You were looking at *me* earlier." He crossed his arms, knowing he had won the argument, judging by the triumphant gleam in his eyes.

"The book, please?" Beatrix shifted the topic of conversation.

"Here." He easily reached the book's spine and removed it to the point of where it was teetering on the edge.

"You simply could not resist, could you?" Beatrix grumbled as she reached and pulled out the book.

"No," he answered honestly, "but to be honest… if you were in my position, would you have done any different?"

"No… wait. Yes."

He cocked his head, waiting.

"I would have tried to make the book fall on your head," Beatrix replied then dashed across the room.

"Unbelievable!" he called out and gave chase.

"You're simply jealous I thought of it rather than you." She spoke as she strategically stepped, placing the chaise between them.

"I'd never do anything so diabolical to a lady," he shot back then slowly circled the chaise.

Beatrix matched him step for step till they'd made a full lap around the piece of furniture.

"This is pointless," he replied, walked away and sat in the chair. He reached for a book on the side table and began reading.

Beatrix watched him for a moment then took a seat as well.

Halfway into the first chapter of her book she glanced up, noticing that Lord Neville was not across from her any longer.

"Lesson one… never let your guard down," he whispered from beside her.

"How did you do that?" she asked, startled that she had missed his movement.

"Shouldn't you be more concerned with why?" he asked.

Beatrix swallowed, trying not to notice how his nearness radiated comforting warmth or how the very air was permeated with a masculine spicy scent that called to her. "Why?"

"In this case… it was the only way I could get close enough to do this," he whispered as he leaned in slightly. His hand reached up and gently placed a lock of hair behind her ear.

"What if… if I don't want you to?" Beatrix asked, knowing full well how much she *did* want him too; however, the last thing she wanted was for him to know that!

"Then simply say no," he murmured, his gaze darting from her lips to her eyes once more. "Are you… going to say no?"

Beatrix blinked, unable to break the swirling fog of desire that wound around them like mist from the sea. "No."

He leaned away, and Beatrix realized the misunderstanding. He had thought she'd meant she didn't welcome his affection!

Quickly, she reached up and placed her hand against his cheek, immediately feeling his warm skin through her glove.

Hope dawned in his expression, and immediately he closed the distance and pressed his lips to hers, caressing them softly.

Longingly.

He withdrew slightly, but only to tilt his head further before placing another kiss to her lips, sliding his across hers softly, invitingly. She reached up and placed her hand at his shoulder, pulling him in closer, a request he immediately obeyed. His kiss deepened, and Beatrix lost herself in the thousands of blissful sensations that were all awakening each moment. She almost gasped when his velvet tongue slid across her lower lip a second before his teeth playfully nipped at it.

Not wanting to be outdone, she tentatively mimicked his actions, glorying in his reaction as her hand at his shoulder felt the telling bunching of his musculature as he leaned in deeper to their shared kiss. With each nip and caress, she gave and took, a constant partner in the dance, moving with the music of desire awakening.

The sound of voices, angry voices, interrupted Beatrix's blissful state and shook her back to the reality of her situation.

She was alone.

With an unmarried gentleman.

Which was enough to consider her compromised, not to mention she had been willingly participating in a far-more-than-chaste kiss.

Heaven's above, Carlotta would have her hide!

As if sensing her thoughts, Neville withdrew. His stormy grey gaze searched her face, memorizing her. "I'm… I shouldn't have." He glanced away, as a cold chill hit her chest. "You are fascinating in a way that is dangerous, Miss Beatrix, and, for that reason, I must leave. Regardless of how… right now… I very much want to stay."

What did one say to that? For that matter, what did one say after a kiss? Speechless, Beatrix nodded, confused.

However, as the voices grew louder, Lord Neville stood

and straightened his jacket then strode to the door.

Beatrix only saw him one other time before he quit the house party they were attending.

Then all thought of stolen kisses and ruined novels faded into the background when the duke received a cryptic threat against her. Though orphaned, she and her sisters, Berty and Bethanny were staggeringly wealthy, not to mention the wards of the Duke of Clairmont. With Bethanny safely married to Lord Graham and Berty still quite young, Beatrix had been left with the target at her back, or so the officer from Scotland Yard had said to the duke.

It had been less than two weeks since the house party, yet it felt like several years. At first, the duke had been told that the death of her parents had not been accidental. Yet, as horrific as such a claim had been, it hadn't added up. Within a few days, another officer had informed them of new evidence that suggested it was a false lead. The only tangible information they could disclose was that Beatrix was a target for *something*.

Helpful.

Each time an officer would come to the door, Beatrix would find herself holding her breath, wondering, fearing.

Enough was enough. So when the duke devised a plan to remove her from the public eye, just to be cautious, she'd agreed. Anything would be better than simply living in fear. No one could know where she traveled. To cover their plan, the duke would claim she'd been taken, kidnapped.

Beatrix thought the whole ordeal overly dramatic, but what could one do?

So she played along, hoping everything would conclude quickly. And, in the meantime, she'd dream about stolen kisses, and try to forget about an evil that lurked in the London shadows.

# CHAPTER ONE

*A year later*

EDWIN ROWLAND, EIGHTH EARL OF NEVILLE, flexed his hands as he gripped the bannister overlooking the small garden of the inn that housed him for the night. The song of the crickets did nothing for his taut nerves. Paradoxically, his heart pounded with a fierce dread and anticipation. There was no sign of her.

It was as if she had vanished. Of their own accord, his fingers bit into the stone railing, grasping for control of something.

Lord only knew how much he needed control right then.

Of anything.

The sun had long set, and the stars twinkled in the ink sky, yet he didn't notice their beauty, only forced his thoughts from the woman he couldn't forget.

A woman he had not known nearly long enough to create such an… attachment.

But that didn't make it less real.

Her ebony hair beckoned for his touch; rather, he burned to test the weight of the unbound tresses. Eyes the color of warm caramel and a smile that was equal parts sass and intelligence haunted him.

And as quick as he'd found her…

She'd been taken.

Life was too ironic. The unwelcome sensation of déjà vu tickled his mind, yet he repressed it.

He'd not think of that now. No, now he needed to focus, to think. Harboring himself in the Fox Inn, he was grasping at straws.

But he had promised, to a duke no less.

And with his experience with the war office, he was truly the best man for the job. London held no lure anyway, not when he knew the price paid to withhold the truth, and when only judgment and a reclusive life waited for him.

As he searched for Beatrix, Miss Lamont, he reminded himself, it was as if life held more purpose, more value. It was a bright temptation to hope once more.

Yet with each day that passed with no sign of her, the bleak realization poured over him anew.

Yet, he'd given his word, and he'd not fail.

He would find her.

"YOU, THERE!" LORD NEVILLE strode toward the stable boy, taking in his smudged face along with the wary look that lit his gaze.

"Aye, Gov'ner." The lad nodded, his blue eyes narrowing in a mix of fear and respect.

"Could you tell me who that horse belongs to?" He nodded to the black mare; her highly arched neck and impatient paw at the ground further affirmed his suspicions. She was a beauty, horseflesh of quality, of money. It was a rarity for gentry to be abiding in such a small inn during the season. Any, *any,* oddity, anything that seemed out of place begged his attention.

"Tha' one? Ach, she's a beauty, sir. A grand lady had ta leave her here, tossed a shoe and came up lame. The stable master, he fixed her up real nice, but the lady left before she was ready to ride. Bought a horse in town, she did."

Lord Neville nodded and turned to the horse. The mare's ears pricked and twisted as she snorted and seemed to wait for his next move. "What did the lady look like?" he asked, keeping his tone slightly disinterested.

"Well… she was a fine one. Fancy dress and all. Smiled too. Had a right pretty girl with her, tho' I suppose 'twas a lady too, the way she spoke and dressed."

"Hmm…" Lord Neville replied, pacing back to the lad. "What did the younger lady look like?" He bent down to the lad's level, watching him.

"Right pretty, sir. Brown hair all tied up like ladies do, and a fine dress like the older lady. They seemed quite happy to be together."

"I see." Lord Neville stood, no longer feeling that he might be onto the trail of the missing woman. He steeled himself as he thought her name: Beatrix.

"Oh! I almost forgot, sir. The older lady, she left this." The stable boy spun and ran to a tack room and disappeared. In a moment, he returned with a small square of linen.

He reached out and accepted it from the stable boy. The trim around the edges was feminine, delicate. But it was the initials embroidered into the corner that confused him.

*SR*

Keeping his face impassive, he folded the linen and stuffed it into his greatcoat pocket. "Thanks, lad." He withdrew a coin and tossed it to the boy, who caught it midair and grinned.

"Thank you!" He scrambled off, clutching the coin tightly in his fist.

The dark horse nickered behind him, and Lord Neville glanced behind him, narrowing his eyes and studying the animal once more. A suspicion crept along his mind, and he turned, leaving the hay-rich stable behind and choosing to cross the worn dirt street.

The Fox Chase Tavern was only a moment's walk, and in little time, he entered the dimly lit establishment. The air was thick with the scent of spilled ale and earthy humanity. Once his eyes adjusted, he took a seat near the bar keep, signaling for an ale.

After taking a sip of the stout brew, he waved at the tender.

The portly gentleman ambled over to him, a slight limp to his stride. He leaned up on the bar and raised his bushy white eyebrows. "Aye?"

"My aunt has a cottage around these parts, but my coachman is ill, and I'm needing to find her residence on my own. Could you please direct me to the estate of Lady Southridge?" Lord Neville kept his gaze open, knowing he was taking a long shot in the dark.

"Southridge, eh? Well, ye aren't too far from it. If ye take Kippen Road out of town, you'll follow it till ye hit the tree line, walnut trees, I believe. Past that is the gate to Breckridge House." He nodded once and stood straight. After wiping his hands on a towel at the bar, he left to attend another patron.

*Southridge.*

What in the hell was he supposed to do with that information? Of course he was going to pay a visit to the Lady Southridge at her estate, but would Beatrix be there?

Safe and sound?

*Not* kidnapped?

Simply… taken without informing anyone?

Though Lord Neville wasn't too familiar with Lady Southridge, the rumors of her unorthodox behavior made him accept the possibility that this, indeed, was possibly the case in Beatrix's situation.

But what then?

Dear heavens above, he had to tell the duke.

The duke who viewed Lady Southridge as a maternal figure.

Could the day get worse?

Bloody betraying lot, all of them! This was why he avoided London, the whole season of the misbegotten *ton*.

It was a nightmare — a pox on them all!

Regardless, he was under obligation to ferret out the truth. He had promised.

And he never went back on his word.

Ever.

"Isn't the sunshine lovely?" Beatrix Lamont fanned herself slightly with her white-gloved hand as she walked along the stone path toward the orangery.

"There's nothing sweeter than sunshine after such miserable rain," Lady Southridge affirmed, her green eyes crinkling as she gave Beatrix a warm smile.

Beatrix inhaled deeply, thankful for the fresh and crisp air of the English Countryside. It was a stark contrast to the stench and smoke-hazed air of London. After all, she and her sisters had been raised near Bath, close enough to the sea that the slight flavor of salt lingered in the air.

A lingering fear clenched in her heart as she momentarily thought over the reasons for her exile from London. As stagnant as the air was in town, it was still in a way, home. It was there she'd found a new place to belong with her guardian, the Duke of Clairmont and his wife, Carlotta. Pushing those thoughts aside, she let her gaze linger on the gardens of Breckridge House. It was a pleasure to enjoy the soft incline of the hills and the smattering of trees that lined the long drive. Not a horizon filled with stone buildings, but pure nature.

"It's a beautiful view, is it not?" Lady Southridge's voice pulled her from the abandon of the scenery.

"Indeed," Beatrix murmured.

"And you're safe here, Beatrix. You're safe." Lady Southridge's tone took on a protective edge, a fierceness that was familiar, yet foreign. For, while the older woman was indeed fierce, it was usually in some misbegotten meddling scheme… nothing quite as serious as protecting Beatrix's very life.

"I know." Beatrix sucked in a tight breath, not willing to dwell on the what ifs that plagued her at night…

But failing to keep her imagination in check.

"No one knows… rather… no one that needs to know knows… if that makes sense."

Beatrix glanced to her, watching as a confused expression darkened her green eyes before she waved her hand. "But I do apologize for the need for your disguise… it goes against the grain for me to set you up as a bluestocking in the house." She shook her head slightly, her silvering reddish hair not moving from its perfect design under her straw bonnet.

"I understand. Besides, a lady's companion isn't exactly arduous work." Beatrix shook her head in amusement.

"Well… you've not been in my employ for long," Lady Southridge shot back, grinning.

"True. Yet, I find I'm unable to summon the proper amount of trepidation for my position," Beatrix quipped.

"Such cheek! Don't you know you cannot speak to your betters in such a way?" Lady Southridge feigned insult a moment before a grin broke through her attempt at a stern glare.

"Yes, ma'am. A thousand apologies," Beatrix murmured, bowing a curtsey and averting her gaze.

Lady Southridge's snort broke through her facade of humility, and she grinned in spite of herself.

"You do that, and I'll set you up as a scullery maid," the

older woman threatened.

Beatrix glanced up to her annoyed expression. Her lips were pressed together tightly, as if trying to hold back laughter.

Her hypothesis was proven true when Lady Southridge glanced away, chuckling. "I do give you credit for your acting abilities, my dear."

"Thank you." Beatrix took a moment to bow.

"That being said, I've not told a soul in the house's employ the truth of the situation. As far as they are all concerned, you are Beverly Blithe, my companion. I breeched conduct when I put you in a room above stairs, but when I explained to Miss Meecham about the need for you to be close, it seemed to satisfy that gleam of curiosity in her beady eyes."

"Lady Southridge!" Beatrix scolded, biting back a giggle.

She paused in her relaxed amble and placed her hands on her hips as she focused on Beatrix. "Are you to say you disagree with my observation?" she dared.

Beatrix narrowed her eyes back, pausing. "No… but to say such things… why… it's simply rude."

"It's not rude if it's the truth. The woman does have beady eyes," Lady Southridge shot back. "But I see your point, which is why I will refrain from telling her."

"How noble of you," Beatrix replied cheekily.

"I rather think so."

They continued their walk and approached the orangery door. The large stone building was eggshell-white with stone corbels surrounding the upper perimeter, adding functionality and design. The windows faced south, spreading out before them as they approached the heavy wooden door. Lady Southridge twisted the handle, and it opened without so much as a creak. Immediately the scent of fertile earth and humid moisture assaulted Beatrix, comforting her, calling to her. The Orangery was easily her favorite place at Breckridge house.

They passed several stone benches facing the windows

that were filtering in the light. The sound of their skirts swishing seemed overly loud in the peaceful setting, but only for a moment as Lady Southridge began speaking. Silence wasn't her strong point.

"I love it here. So peaceful."

Beatrix bit back a laugh. How like Lady Southridge, needing to break the silence by speaking of it.

"Indeed. But I must say that my favorite part is the far corner." Beatrix nodded her head toward the back alcove.

"Mine too…" Lady Southridge agreed then turned to Beatrix, a sparkle in her green eyes. "Had I been able to have children, I dare say they would have been conceived in that very alcove."

Beatrix gasped then felt her face flame in a blush. "And to think the duke set me in your care… the scandal you speak of," she teased.

"You've known me far too long to be scandalized by anything I say." Lady Southridge waved her off. "Regardless, it *is* quite the romantic corner. Just don't let me find you using it," she warned.

"Because there are so many gentleman around here?" Beatrix glanced around the vacant orangery meaningfully.

"Not at all, but nevertheless, what type of guardian would I be if I didn't speak my piece?" She shrugged.

"No… since we have a moment, let us discuss the particulars."

"I'm quite sure I'm aware of the particulars of my situation, Lady Southridge," Beatrix replied, her tone betraying her exasperation. Hadn't they discussed this enough?

"No, I don't think I can articulate enough the need for you to be completely aware of all this entails. This is for your own protection. You're very life… we cannot afford to take it lightly.

"Very well." Beatrix sobered and turned her full attention

to Lady Southridge

The older woman gestured to a stone bench that lined the wall. "Now… because I'm in residence, there will be people who will stop by and wish to visit with me. As my companion, you'll need to make an appearance so that it will not cause some sort of mystery. Heaven only knows that mystery only makes people curious and stupid. Especially the *ton*. Therefore, you'll be introduced as my companion and then fully ignored by any that come to visit. When a lady enters the room, you'll set aside your embroidery, stand and nod, then sit and become as invisible as possible. When you are introduced, keep your head down. I'll have Mary hide as much of your glorious hair as possible." Her forehead creased as she reached out and touched Beatrix's head. "It might take some work, but I believe we can hide it under mobcap — not necessarily the fashion or even becoming for a companion — but it will be a necessary aid in this deception". She nodded. "And I do believe we'll put you in mourning colors… perhaps."

"Pardon?" Beatrix asked as she felt her jaw drop.

"Mourning colors… not the black of the first year… no, that will cause scandal… but maybe the muted colors of a widow in her second year? Yes, that will do nicely." She gave a sharp nod of approval to her own plan. "We'll also be sure you're covered up completely… maybe add a pillow here or there…" Lady Southridge tilted her head and placed her hand on her chin, evaluating.

"No. I draw the line at pillows. Next I'll be an… expectant mother as well." Beatrix shook her head.

"No, no, nothing so drastic. My dear, don't be dramatic." Lady Southridge tsked her tongue.

Beatrix narrowed her eyes. Yes… because *she* was being the dramatic one.

"It will be like a game!" Lady Southridge exclaimed, clapping her hands and startling Beatrix.

"Yes… a game," Beatrix replied, unable to procure the same amount of enthusiasm.

"Oh posh, don't be so sour! You at least get to spend time with me," Lady Southridge remarked, grinning.

"True." And Beatrix *was* glad to spend time with her.

"Now… I suggest you enjoy your last day before we start the ruse." Lady Southridge spoke kindly as she stood and straightened her skirt. "I don't expect anyone will visit before tomorrow—"

Lady Southridge was interrupted by the sound of someone's entrance to the orangery. A maid glanced about and spotted them. With hurried steps she approached and curtseyed. "My lady, you have a caller. Trent tried to send him away, but he… well, he refused."

"Refused?"

Beatrix watched Lady Southridge's eyes widen in concern. "What exactly do you mean, Polly?" She narrowed her eyes slightly.

Polly glanced to the cobblestone floor and shifted her weight nervously. "I… that is… he was insistent and mentioned that you had left something at the Fox Inn that you'd wish returned. He refused to leave the item with Trent."

Lady Southridge sighed heavily. Turning to Beatrix, she placed her hands on her hips. "So much for our plans. Beverly? Would you please ask cook to prepare tea? We'll take it in my private chambers."

Beatrix nodded in understanding. *Beverly.* So that was going to be her name for the time being. Well, it could be worse, she decided. "Of course, my lady." Beatrix slipped into her role and curtseyed, but as she turned to leave, Lady Southridge's voice stopped her.

"Bev? Please, enjoy the orangery for just a few minutes and then be sure to slip through the servants' entrance I showed you earlier. It will take you directly to cook." Lady Southridge's gaze was direct and shrewd, as if trying to convey additional meaning to her words.

Beatrix understood immediately. Wait first then slip inside unnoticed.

*And so it begins.*

At least she wasn't wearing the mobcap yet!

"Come, Polly. Let's go see what the ruckus is all about. I can't imagine what I left…" Lady Southridge's voice trailed off as she left with Polly.

Beatrix sighed and glanced around the vacant orangery. She walked down an aisle of potted lemon trees, reaching out and brushing leaves with her hands. Trying to ignore the cold finger of fear that tickled her heart, she tried to reason with herself. It was nigh too impossible for someone to know she had taken to hiding with Lady Southridge. It was simply a coincidence that had brought some strange gentleman to the door of Breckridge House.

When she was there…

Hiding.

Dear heavens… she needed to stop this!

Taking a deep breath, she squared her shoulders and walked over to the door. It pushed open silently and spilled in the sunshine. Her fears melting in the warmth, she walked around the back of the orangery and toward the servants' entrance.

It was a plain wooden door and opened directly into the kitchen area of Breckridge House. Immediately the sounds of the bustling kitchen met her ears. As she rounded the stone wall, she paused at the sound of cook yelling at the scullery maid. A river of runny eggs and shattered shells dotted the wooden floor of the kitchen. A loud thud startled her as a young lad slipped on the mess, dropping his wooden bucket in the process and sending cook into another fit. Leaning back against the cool stone wall, she watched as several maids rushed forward with rags and another bucket. Beatrix paused, waiting till cook's color returned to a safer shade of pink, rather than the angry crimson that had flushed her face earlier. Clearing her throat softly, she straightened her posture away from the wall.

"Aye?" The plump woman glanced to Beatrix. Her mobcap skewed slightly with a few grey curls peeking through. Her blue eyes narrowed impatiently then softened.

"Lady Southridge requests tea served in her private chambers." Beatrix nodded slightly.

"Very well." Cook turned toward the stove, but not before glaring once again at the mess on the floor.

Sidestepping the remaining river of eggs, Beatrix made her way to the stairs that would lead to the back of the house. If she were careful, she could make it from the servants' quarters to the staircase leading to Lady Southridge's chambers without being seen.

She'd simply be cautious.

And thus was now the story of her life.

# CHAPTER TWO

NEVILLE TAPPED HIS FOOT IMPATIENTLY AS he stared daggers at the bloody butler who had all but assaulted him with a cane.

As if sensing his thoughts, the butler jerked the cane.

Neville narrowed his eyes further, daring him to try something.

He wanted to pick a fight.

Even if it was with a bloody octogenarian butler with a wicked cane.

Footsteps in the hall pulled his attention, and he glanced from the butler to the door of the parlor where he waited.

Lady Southridge entered with a flourish of grey and emerald, an impatient expression on her face that immediately changed into one of recognition. "Lord Neville?"

"Ah, Lady Southridge." He stood and bowed, sliding his gaze to the evil butler in triumph.

"What in heaven's name are you doing here?" Lady Southridge asked.

He was about to reply when he was interrupted by a cough from the butler.

A cough that sounded suspiciously like a laugh.

He cast a threatening glare to the old codger then turned back to Lady Southridge. "It's quite simple actually. I was staying at the same inn as you, apparently, for I came to return some misplaced items. One of which is your fine horse." He tilted his head, watching her reaction, studying it.

"Oh… well, I thank you. There was no need for you to go to such trouble," she replied coolly.

"And this." He withdrew the handkerchief and held it out for her.

"Oh… again, how kind." Her gaze narrowed.

And even a man of his merit felt the urge to squirm under her scrutiny.

"Aren't you quite the gentleman for taking such an… interest… in this?" she replied.

"It was nothing of the sort. I simply found them while searching for something else," Lord Neville replied, testing the waters.

"Were you able to find that which you were searching for?" she asked, still spearing him with her green gaze.

"Not yet. But I do believe I'm rather close."

"Indeed." Lady Southridge shrugged. "Would you care for tea?"

He tugged on his white gloves. "Tea would be delightful."

"Trent? Would you please notify cook of a change of plans? I'll take my tea here with Lord Neville."

"Of course, my lady." The butler stood, the movement punctuated by the sound his cane hitting the marbled floor with more force than necessary.

Lady Southridge glanced to him curiously at the loud thud.

"Quite the help you have here," Lord Neville spoke as the butler left.

"Loyal to a fault." She gave him a pointed glare. "Please, sit, Lord Neville." Lady Southridge invited, gesturing to a seat across from the one she had just chosen.

"Apparently," Neville spoke under his breath.

"Hmm?"

"Nothing, nothing. So, Lady Southridge, what brings you to Breckridge House? And in the middle of the season? I do hope you are feeling well."

"Quite well. Thank you for your concern. But you see, with my brother just married to the lovely Bethanny, I do think they require some privacy. Wouldn't you agree?"

"Indeed. However, I'm afraid I'm the bearer of bad tidings then. I can only assume by your mannerisms that you have not heard." He leaned forward in his chair and folded his hands carefully. He was wary to make his expression severely concerned, even preparing to lower his tone.

"What tidings?" Lady Southridge's mannerisms were alert, disturbed.

"It would seem that one of the wards of the Duke of Clairmont, one of Bethanny's sisters, has been abducted," he whispered.

"No!" Lady Southridge immediately stood, her hand fanning herself wildly. "No, it cannot be! How was I not informed?" She walked around the chair then gripped the back carefully.

"Indeed." He nodded once.

"How is poor Bethanny doing? And Charles? Oh heavens! I must leave for London at once! But oh! I cannot!" She placed her hand to her forehead as if about to faint.

"Are you ill?" Lord Neville stood, feeling trepidation that the woman might actually faint. Dear Lord, heaven only knew what the butler would do with the cane then!

"No... no." She took in a few steadying breaths... "I'm well. Quite... well," she answered and squared her shoulders. "You must find her!" she all but commanded.

"My lady, why do you think I'm gallivanting about the English countryside?" he asked.

"Well, how am I to know if you're on holiday or not?

What *are* you doing, Lord Neville?" She placed her hands on her hips and narrowed her gaze.

"Trying to find her. And… I might add…" He took a step toward her, meeting her gaze. "…I was told something quite interesting while at the Fox Inn." He let his words linger as he watched her expression for the smallest sign of avoidance. "You see… the stable boy was quite impressed with the beauty of your traveling partner…" He took another step closer, letting the statement hang heavily in the air.

Then she laughed.

"He thought Bev was a beauty? Well, I'll have to tell her that! It should make her day, being widowed these years." She shook her head.

"Bev?" Lord Neville continued to watch her. Her laughter had taken him by surprise, but it held an edge to the sound… slightly unnatural… which kept his interest.

"Yes, Bev. My lady's companion. A very shy thing, but great for keeping an old woman like me company." She waved her hand dismissively.

"And just where did you hire Bev?" He asked, hearing skepticism lace his tone.

"In London, of course. Lady Crumpton's daughter's governess knew of a woman's son who had lost his life at sea, leaving a poor widow. Of course, she was from a prominent family but had… well, married beneath her. Ah, the things the heart does for love." She seemed to lose herself in the story as she sighed heavily and gazed into the air.

"Lady Southridge?" he called, resisting the urge to snap his fingers in front of her face. He was growing impatient.

"Oh, dear me. A thousand apologies. What was I saying?" she asked, all innocent and kind.

Neville took a calming breath. "You were telling the dramatic tale of your lady's companion," he clipped out.

"Indeed. Poor Bev… all alone, not a shilling to her name. Well, I simply *had* to take her in, you see."

"Of course." He narrowed his eyes. "Being such a close acquaintance."

"Do not mock me, young man," Lady Southridge snapped, her green eyes igniting like fire.

"I'd never dream of such a thing, my lady," he replied, bowing somberly and returning to his seat, his skin all but crawling with the suspicion that she was simply putting on a ruse.

"Of course, it's been a hard transition for her, being here… which is another reason why we left London… too many memories."

"Of her husband?" Neville asked, growing amused by her long tale in spite of himself.

"No… didn't I mention he was a sailor?" She cocked her head and pressed a finger to her chin. "Yes, I do believe I mentioned that. Do try to keep up, Lord Neville," she scolded.

"I—"

"And do not interrupt."

He nodded, biting back a wry grin.

"Now… London was where she was raised… because, if you'll remember my story, she was from a wealthy family and simply… followed her heart."

"How tragic," he replied stoically.

"Ah! No, how *romantic.*"

"Yes, this whole story is quite the story of love." He was growing weary.

"Regardless, I shall not bore you with the details. We should not lose sight of what is important, and *that* is that you should find Beatrix." She nodded, strode to her seat, and sat with a decisive nod.

"I do believe I was trying to explain that it is, indeed, my intention to find her. Since my news came as such a shock to you, I assume you have no idea where she could have gone?" he asked.

"Hmm…" Lady Southridge's lips twisted slightly, as she

appeared to think. "I do not think she'd travel to Greenford Waters on her own… and if she was taken as you say… then I'm afraid I am no help. But I must urge you onward to find her! You must not linger a single moment." She stood and waved at him to stand as well. "You must go. Now."

"Lady Southridge, I appreciate your enthusiasm, but I was going to beg a favor of you." Neville watched as she gave one final longing glace at the door then turned her eyes to him. "Would it be possible to impose on you for a few days so that I might search this area? I've visited a few inns, but I do believe I can find out more information if I'm not… shall we say… traveling as a gentleman." He lowered his chin and speared her with his gaze.

"Is that so?" Lady Southridge queried skeptically.

"Indeed. I have exhausted all other options, and I'm getting rather desperate." He took a step toward her, keeping his expression open and hopeful. What he really wanted was to be allowed access to Breckridge House… because he was quite certain that Bev, the lady's maid, was Beatrix, kidnapped ward of the duke. But what he couldn't figure out was *why* Lady Southridge had done it.

"I do believe I can help you… but I must insist that you do not stay overly long. My lady's maid… well, she gets rather shy around men, and I do not wish her to be uncomfortable."

"Thank you, Lady Southridge. Your hospitality is appreciated. I will not overstay my welcome." He bowed.

Her gaze narrowed as she studied him. Cautiously, she stood and went to ring the bell. "Trent will show you to a room."

"Delightful," he spoke then swore inwardly. Yes, that bloody butler would show him to a room with a view… off a cliff.

"If you'll excuse me then, I do believe I'll take a moment to refresh myself." She glanced to the door, and he could practically hear the churning of her mind as she bustled toward it.

"Here's your tea, my lady." Polly arrived just as Lady Southridge tried to make her escape.

"Ah, thank you. Please set it on the table there and serve Lord Neville." She turned to face him. "I'll be back down in a moment to join you."

With that, she left.

After the maid served him tea, he sipped the hot and bitter liquid, letting it warm him. There was some sort of mayhem afoot, and he was going to discover exactly what it was.

First order of business, find Bev — or Beatrix — whoever she truly was.

"BEV!" LADY SOUTHRIDGE'S VOICE echoed in her private chambers and startled Beatrix so much she dropped her book.

"Yes? Heavens, what is going on?" Her heart pumped wildly. Was there danger? Had someone already discovered her hiding place?

"Damn the man," Lady Southridge swore as she paced madly in front of the fire.

"Pardon?" Beatrix tilted her head as she studied her.

"It would seem that the reclusive Lord Neville picked a delightful day to come out of hiding… and his target would be no one other than you, my dear." She heaved a sigh of irritation.

"Lord Neville?" Beatrix felt goose flesh prickle her skin at the thought of the reclusive lord and the secret they shared.

"The one and only… downstairs and all but demanding to stay here while he looks for you."

"He's looking for me?" Her heart beat wildly. Lord Neville, looking for her? Was he concerned? Wait… why would he be searching for her? He wasn't Scotland Yard.

"Yes! Hadn't I said that?" Her shoulders slumped.

"Pardon, my dear. I'm sorry I snapped at you."

"Don't fret. I'll simply stay in my room, or your room… whatever room a lady's maid is to be in," she amended and walked over to where Lady Southridge stood gazing out the picture window facing the back garden. "But I am confused."

"Hmm?" Lady Southridge turned slightly to face her. Green eyes full of concern helped alleviate some of Beatrix's tension.

"I… that is… why would Lord Neville search for me? We are not well acquainted, and rather, I find it odd that he'd even know I'm missing." Glancing down, she pulled at the fingertips of her gloves and bit her lip.

"Ah, I guess the gossip hasn't reached every corner of London yet."

"Pardon?" Beatrix's met Lady Southridge's gaze.

"It's quite the story, you know. Lord Neville wasn't always a recluse."

"He's not exactly a recluse now," Beatrix felt the need to add.

"True, I do find it strange that he's come out of hiding recently." Lady Southridge's brow creased. "Of course there was a whisper that he was considering your sister, Bethanny, at one point." She tilted her head thoughtfully.

Beatrix bit back the quick pang of jealousy, reminding herself that her sister had never had eyes for anyone other than Lord Graham, now her husband.

"But, of course, that was an exercise in futility. Bethanny was going to marry my brother if she had to kidnap him." Lady Southridge chuckled then paused. "Poor choice of words, my dear. So sorry." She reached out and patted Bethanny's shoulder.

"Perhaps, if I actually *were* kidnapped." Beatrix grinned.

"True, true… but I digress. Lord Neville. Hmm… you have, of course, heard the rumors that he killed his betrothed?"

Beatrix rolled her eyes. "I haven't heard *all* the gossip, but I have heard enough to know that particular story is a farce if I've ever heard one."

"You always were a clever girl."

"I don't believe my seeing through such a gossip points to my cleverness. Rather, I think that my believing such a wild tale would rather point to my intense lack of intellect."

"And so you condemn half the *ton?*" Lady Southridge spoke questioningly.

"You would vouch for them otherwise?" Beatrix speared her with a knowing gaze.

"No. I would not."

Beatrix nodded in victory.

"Be that as it may… Lord Neville took to his reclusive state after his betrothed passed. He was never convicted of any crime, and I, myself, would be utterly shocked if he had anything to do with her demise. However, stranger things have happened." She shook her head slightly. "But Lord Neville has a few secrets that the *ton* doesn't gossip about."

"Oh?" Beatrix leaned in slightly, waiting.

"Lord Neville is not what he seems to be. I'm not sure if it was brilliant or bloody idiotic for your guardian, the duke, to send him after you… but it will alleviate any questions concerning your reputation."

"Wh—"

"Let me finish," Lady Southridge interrupted.

"Lord Neville has worked for the crown here and there — not much, mind you — but enough to earn enough notoriety and respect that people will not question the validity of the duke's story of your kidnapping, especially when he mentions Lord Neville searching for you. In other words, my dear, when the *ton* gossips about you, it will be because of what the duke has told them, not because of what they are making up." She tilted her chin down spearing him with a direct gaze, as if trying to convey something silently.

"I'm… afraid I'm not following."

"Innocent girl." Lady Southridge shook her head. "It's the end of the season. Why would a girl disappear suddenly?"

"Because… she was kidnapped? Got ill? I don't know."

"Because she needed to…" Lady Southridge glanced down and patted her very flat stomach.

Beatrix felt her eyes widen. "They'd think I was…" She let the word linger, not comfortable with staying it aloud.

"Quicker than a rake's wink."

"Dear heavens."

"Which is why I'm starting to believe that it was a stroke of genius for the duke to send Lord Neville after you. However, now we must deal with the man." Lady Southridge began to pace about the room, her slippered feet making a slight muted thump on the wooden floor.

"Why don't we just tell him?" Beatrix asked, finding the solution quite simple.

Lady Southridge spun on her heel and glared. "Because you're in hiding."

"And he can't keep a secret?" Beatrix replied archly.

"I… er… well, I'm sure he could, but this is not his secret to keep." Lady Southridge nodded and returned to her pacing. "Besides, in order to keep your reputation pristine, a gentleman cannot be in residence."

"He wouldn't have to *be* in residence. He could go on his merry way once he knows the truth and continue the farce of looking for me."

"If he believed you were here of your own accord… but he doesn't believe you are. The duke sent him after you. Just *whom* do you think he'll believe? Me or the duke?"

"Drat… I see your point."

"Exactly."

"And if he's off searching the countryside, it makes it look like you truly cannot be found, and that, my dear, makes you much safer." Lady Southridge paused her pacing and glanced to the window. When she turned her gaze back to Beatrix, her eyes were glassy, as if restraining tears.

Beatrix swallowed whatever words she was about to say. It was easy to pretend the whole situation was a game, but in that moment she was reminded that it was, indeed, not a game.

But far too real.

Someone wanted something she didn't even know she had.

There could be no mistakes.

"I'll wear a disguise and hide in my chamber. He'll stay no more than a week, and we'll be done with the whole business," Beatrix spoke decisively.

"I don't see how we have any other choice." Lady Southridge took a fortifying breath and squared her shoulders. "I need to return to the parlor, but I had to let you know what was taking place. Do *not* leave this room." She pointed at a chair, as if commanding her to sit, and then strode with purpose-filled steps to the door. "Oh, and before I forget the story, I told him your name is Bev, and I hired you in London as a lady's companion."

Beatrix nodded. They had been over this.

"And you are the widow of a sailor who was the acquaintance of Lady Compton's daughter's governess's friend."

"Pardon?" Beatrix blinked.

"Perhaps I went too elaborate, but I didn't want him to be able to trace anything." She placed a finger at her chin. "I'll simply have to write it down for you to memorize, just in case." She nodded then left in a flurry of skirts.

"Lady Compton's what?" Beatrix breathed. If *that* story was what Lady Southridge had come up with on short notice, heaven help them *all* if the woman had put any amount of thought into it!

Well, there was nothing to do but wait.

Which surprisingly was a trait she rather prized about herself.

It wasn't glorious, it wasn't awe-inspiring, but it was rather useful. She could wait. She could be patient and, over the years with her sisters, it had proved to serve her well more than once.

Much to Bethanny's and Berty's chagrin.

As her mind drifted to her sisters, her heart prickled with a pang of loneliness. Yes, she was quite smothered with love from Lady Southridge, but with sisters, it was a different type of love. There was a comradery, a give and take and all-around drama that made life so… well… not boring.

And secure, all at once.

It was true that her oldest sister Bethanny now had her husband, Lord Graham, but that was the rub. They had always had each other — as it should be — but Beatrix had left shortly after, and where did that leave Berty? Alone.

Beatrix held in a chuckle at the thought of Carlotta—their guardian, the duke's wife—who had the arduous task of trying to educate Berty in the ways of a lady. Poor Carlotta was probably about to pull out her hair by this point.

A lesser woman might not survive the whirlwind that was Berty.

Beatrix strode to the window and placed her hand on the cool glass. As much as she missed her sisters, it was worth it to protect them.

Now if she could only control the fluttering of her heart whenever she thought of the handsome man downstairs… the very gentleman she had to avoid at all costs.

Especially when all she wanted to do was the exact opposite.

# CHAPTER THREE

LORD NEVILLE TUGGED ON HIS CRAVAT as Trenton opened the door to the guestroom he'd be using while staying with Lady Southridge. The room was neat and clean, finished in navy and sky blues with a large bed dominating the corner of the room. Light spilled through sheer curtains that were accented by heavy draperies on either side of the windows. There was no fire in the hearth, but the room was tolerably comfortable in spite of that fact.

"Will there be anything else, my lord?" Trenton's voice broke through Neville's inspection of his lodgings.

"No." He turned to the elderly man.

The butler narrowed his eyes slightly, regarding him coolly.

Neville raised an eyebrow in query. But Trenton simply huffed and left.

All his life, Lord Neville had thought of butlers as emotionless, opinionless, and invisible. Of course, he been lucky to find the only one in England that was capable of intense hatred. Of him.

Bloody blessed day.

His misfortune continued into the next several days as his unfruitful search proved more and more vexing with each passing moment. He had scoured the gardens, investigated the stables, and asked servants, all the while pretending to hunt the countryside. The whole bloody farce was wretched, yet he saw no other option available.

Yet.

He was beginning to think this Bev character was a bloody ghost.

Or simply part of Lady Southridge's imagination.

Which was why he'd demand to see her.

It was supper, and, as was polite, Neville joined his hostess for the meal. Upon making mention that he'd never met the illusive Bev, he tried a more direct approach.

"Lady Southridge, I do believe it is imperative that I meet with your lady's maid, especially since she was in London at the time of Beatrix's abduction."

"Lord Neville…" Lady Southridge barely glanced up from her soup. "…I do believe we've already discussed the shy nature of my lady's maid. I'll not have you interrogating her," she replied succinctly.

"It's a matter of great import, Lady Southridge."

"Do you think I have not already questioned the poor girl?" Lady Southridge's green eyes flashed irritation as she speared him with a gaze.

"Of course you have. I wouldn't expect any less. However… you may not have asked the correct questions."

"And you would?"

"Undoubtedly."

"The answer is still no."

"Are you hiding something?" Neville asked, his tone steely smooth.

"How dare you accuse me, in my house—"

"I did not accuse, I simply inquired," Neville replied, keeping his tone polite.

Lady Southridge glared at him then set her spoon down. "Very well. You'll meet Bev, and afterward I'll expect you to continue your search… elsewhere. Agreed?" she asked, placing her hands on her lap, her gaze direct.

"Agreed." He lifted his napkin and set it aside, nodding once. Finally. He took a deep breath. "I'll look forward to making her acquaintance. Tonight." Neville offered a smile toward Lady Southridge, but she didn't return it; rather, took a long sip of wine.

Which, to him, spoke volumes.

"BLOODY HELL."

Beatrix about dropped her book as Lady Southridge burst into the room swearing like a sailor.

"Pardon?"

"You may never speak those words, my dear. Pretend that I did not either," Lady Southridge spoke sternly as she strode to Beatrix' wardrobe and began rummaging through it.

"Can I help you?" Beatrix stood while carefully evaluating the odd behavior of Lady Southridge.

"Yes, no… wait."

Beatrix felt her mouth drop open as Lady Southridge withdrew a deep mud-colored dress. "I do not remember that…" she replied as Lady Southridge studied the ugly garment approvingly.

"Oh, yes… I know. I had Molly put it in here just in case. I do think it will be perfect. Here, put it on." Lady Southridge brought the dress closer, and, with each step, the hideous nature of the dress grew.

"Have I no other option?" Beatrix asked carefully, feeling the need to take a step back with every step Lady Southridge took toward her.

"No. We have no other choice. Lord Neville is all but

insinuating that I'm hiding something from him. All because you—the Bev-you—has not made an appearance. And, while I'm perfectly fine with him questioning my sanity, the bloody man won't leave till he sees you! So, see you, he must. Now, turn. I'll ring for Molly, but I'll get us started."

Beatrix closed her eyes and turned. After the tinkling of the bell, she felt the chilled fingers of Lady Southridge begin to tug at the buttons on the back of her day dress.

"My lady! Allow me to assist," Molly's voice interrupted a few minutes later as Lady Southridge was just finishing.

In short order, the dreadful garment was buttoned up. When Molly finished, Beatrix glared at her reflection in the mirror. While the cut of the dress wasn't atrocious, the color certainly was. The hue was the same exact shade of prune syrup if it were mixed with mud. Neither a purple nor a brown, the dress simply made the statement of ugly without any effort.

"Perfect." Lady Southridge breathed.

"Odd, but I have the exact opposite reaction," Beatrix shot back.

"Now... Molly, do you have the silvering?"

"Pardon?" Beatrix felt her eyes widen. This was *not* part of the plan. "I'm going to be grey?"

"No, dear!" Lady Southridge replied with a cheerful grin.

Beatrix sighed heavily in relief.

"You're simply going to have a few distinguishing streaks of silver."

"No. No, I refuse." Beatrix picked up the hem of her skirts and began to walk away from Molly as she approached her with some sort of cream and a brush.

"You must! I said you were old!"

"That was not on the character description!" Beatrix replied, taking evasive steps from the approaching Molly.

"Oh good! You memorized it then," Lady Southridge replied, a pleased tone to her voice.

"Of course I did. I've had nothing to do for the past three days!"

"Beatrix... he will recognize you immediately if we don't do somethi—"

"I'll wear a veil," she spoke in desperation. And it truly was brilliant because there was no way in heaven or earth that she wanted Lord Neville to see her in *this* dress.

"Oh... a veil would work nicely. You may put away the silvering, Molly."

The maid placed the lid on the container, but Beatrix didn't take a step toward either woman till the vial was put away. Just in case.

"You'll need to lower your voice as well," Lady Southridge instructed as she pulled out a sheer layer of black veil from a trunk in the corner of the room.

"What else have you hidden in my room?" Beatrix asked skeptically.

"Oh, this and that."

"Ah." Beatrix eyed the veil and then glanced about the room.

"We must make haste. He's expecting us."

"Why so soon?" Beatrix asked as they arranged the veil about her face.

"Because it lends the air of transparency."

"Says the woman wrapping a veil around my head," Beatrix replied with a hint of sarcasm.

Lady Southridge smacked her shoulder. "If I made him wait till tomorrow, then he'd suspect something—"

"Because *this* dress and *that* veil aren't a disguise at all."

"Impertinent child! Let me finish. If we have you come down to meet him on demand, it makes it seem like there's nothing we're trying to hide. Now, let me take a good look at you."

Beatrix sighed and waited.

"Very good." Lady Southridge tugged on her hand and

led her out of the room.

The hall was much darker with the thick veil over her face. The material was sheer enough that she could see through it but dark enough that her features were hidden in shadow. Hopefully, that would be enough.

"He's waiting in the red parlor," Lady Southridge spoke in hushed tones. "And remember, don't speak unless absolutely necessary… and then either whisper, and I'll translate, or lower your voice."

"Yes, ma'am," Beatrix spoke contritely, like a proper lady's companion. In a way, it was thrilling to play a part, to be in on the secret; it helped alleviate the tension the truth of the situation lent.

As they approached the door, Lady Southridge turned, studied Beatrix's veil once more, then opened the door.

"Ah, Lord Neville, may I present my lady's companion, Mrs. Beverly Blithe."

Beatrix held her breath. Even through the veil, she could easily discern the cool slate-grey of his eyes, the smart cut of his evening jacket, and the way it accentuated his broad shoulders.

As if reliving the memory of their shape, her hands heated and prickled with awareness, with the intense desire to feel him once more.

He stood and walked over to her, his gaze taking her in, studying her; from the top of her head to the base of her dress.

The bloody, blasted, hideous dress.

That the man didn't wince once was truly notable.

"Ah, we meet at last, Mrs. Blithe." He held out his hand, and Beatrix took it, her body immediately responding with a flash of heat, a flicker of desire.

"She prefers Bev." Lady Southridge interrupted Beatrix's moment, and she tugged at her hand, pulling it from his grasp.

"Very well. Bev, do you speak?" he asked with a tilt to his head. He placed his hands behind his back in a casual manner, but his eyes gave him away.

He knew.

Or he thought he knew.

Dear Lord, how was she ever going to pull this off?

"I speak," Beatrix murmured lowly, barely resisting the urge to clear her throat from the awkward effort of communicating in such a low tone.

Upon hearing her voice, a smirk flashed across his face.

"I'm sure Lady Southridge has communicated to you the reason for my visit here at Breckridge House?" he asked then turned to pace a few steps away.

Beatrix nodded as his sharp gaze flickered to her.

"I feel compelled to ask if you have seen Beatrix Lamont. It is of the utmost importance that I find her." He took at meaningful step toward her.

Beatrix shook her head once more.

"I do apologize for pulling you from your evening, Mrs. — Bev." He nodded once and then turned to Lady Southridge.

"Thank you for so quickly attending to my request. Since I have nothing further to do here at Breckridge House, I do believe I'll take my leave in the morning. Thank you for your hospitality." He bowed once and then left.

Lady Southridge watched his departure then turned to Beatrix, fanning herself as if greatly relieved. They waited in silence for a minute or two then returned to Beatrix's room.

"That was unbelievably simple! I cannot believe how well that worked!" Lady Southridge was all but giddy with enthusiasm, her relief palpable.

"Indeed," Beatrix agreed. But something was off.

Lord Neville was far too… aware of her in the room for him to make such a quick judgment on the negative.

All that night, even amidst Lady Southridge's constant affirmation that they had fooled Lord Neville, Beatrix felt the nagging sensation that they were missing something.

Her tension eased somewhat when Molly notified her of

his departure the next day. She even went as far as watching his chestnut gelding leave the stables. Yet peace was not fully hers, so she decided to take solace in her favorite place in all of Breckridge Estate.

The orangery.

Lady Southridge had offered to accompany her, yet truthfully, she simply wanted some solitude.

So, after securing her bonnet, she made the short jaunt to the welcoming building, inhaling the rich scent of growing botany within. She passed several rows of orange trees, studying their green foliage.

"Good afternoon." Lord Neville's voice broke through the serene silence of the orangery, startling Beatrix and causing her heart to practically take flight. Quickly she spun to face the man speaking, a hand covering her heart as she willed the racing cadence to abate.

His grey eyes took her in with a calculating glint as he lazily stood from his perch on the alcove bench.

There was nothing for it; he knew. It was useless to pretend otherwise. "Hello, Lord Neville. Were the theatrics to your liking?" Beatrix asked with a saucy lilt to her tone as she watched him close the distance.

He clapped slowly, drawing out the gesture. "It might have fooled me…" he replied offhandedly as he shrugged.

"But?" Beatrix asked.

"It was your hands."

"Pardon?" Beatrix asked, confused as she lifted her hands and inspected them.

"When you're nervous, you tend to touch your fingertips to your thumb in succession. It's a telling habit."

"I do?" Beatrix asked as she studied her hands once more then turned her gaze to the man before her.

"Yes."

"How did you know—"

"The library."

Beatrix caught her breath then released it slowly, but she could tell by the spark in his gaze that he hadn't missed her reaction.

Damn the man.

The library… it was nothing. Rather, it should have been nothing.

"Oh." She tried to recover.

His amused chuckle caused her to narrow her eyes, but, rather than show any remorse, his grin grew.

Becoming more devastatingly alluring by the moment.

Heaven help her, but she was helpless against the man. She shouldn't be. There had been just a few stolen moments shared… nothing lasting.

Nothing that should create such a draw.

But it was there, nonetheless.

"You're doing it again." He glanced down to her fingers then met her gaze once more.

Sure enough, she felt her fingers pause as she realized he was indeed correct. How was it that she had never noticed that about herself, yet he, a… well, not a total stranger… had memorized such a nuance?

"Be that as it may…" Beatrix straightened her shoulders and took a few steps to the left, avoiding his direct approach. "…what is it that you want?" she asked in a clipped tone.

"The truth," he replied softly, tilting his head.

"Concerning?" Beatrix asked, taking another side step toward a leafy orange tree.

"Concerning why you're here, of course."

"I would think it's obvious," Beatrix replied loftily as she wound around the orange tree's trunk, keeping an eye on the approaching lord.

Lord Neville clicked his tongue and shook his head, all the while sending her a mischievous grin that melted her insides. "Miss Lamont, we both know that I'm after far more than the obvious… or, in this case… what you wish for me to believe.

I'll warn you that I'm not so easily deterred."

"Oh, is that so?" Beatrix sent him an arch look. "It would seem that you are quite… easily startled," she shot back.

His gaze narrowed as he paused in his approach. "What made you create such an assumption?"

"Why, the library of course." She bit back a grin at the irritated flash in his gaze upon turning the tables back on him.

"The library? Tell me, Miss Lamont, was that before or after I compromised you?" he asked with a dark grin.

"You – oh! You know very well that—"

"That if any matron of society had stumbled into our cozy little interlude you would have been ruined… which was why I walked away. Walked… not ran… as you just implied."

Beatrix bit her lip and glanced away, hating that he was right and had used her shortsighted attempt at victory to turn her own wit against her.

Miserable man.

"You did leave… the next day, that is," she reminded him, watching his expression as it was fixed upon her.

"I did," he replied then took another step toward her.

She placed the tree between them but peeked around the trunk. "Why?" she asked, unable to meet his regard as she spoke.

"Why?" he repeated softly.

Beatrix swallowed her cursed pride and glanced up, compelled by her curiosity to be brave. "Why did you leave so abruptly?"

"For being so expertly compromised—"

"Oh bother." Beatrix rolled her eyes and stepped away, irritated, and gave her back to the lord. "It was a kiss—"

"Perhaps for you…" Lord Neville's hand grasped hers and halted her recession.

Just as she remembered, his hand was warm, enveloping hers completely. A shiver of delighted expectation ripped through her as she slowly turned to face him. Blinking, she waited as his gaze roamed her features and settled on her lips.

"As I was saying… for being so expertly compromised…" Amusement danced in his expression. "…you're truly innocent. I do believe I will have to remedy that," he whispered as he leaned in and brushed a whisper of a kiss across her jaw.

It was as if a thousand butterflies took wing in her belly as she caught the masculine scent of his skin so close to hers. She should reprimand him for taking such liberties…

But she rather liked that he was.

He withdrew and studied her, as if asking if he should continue. Reaching up, Beatrix stroked his jaw, memorizing the texture of his slight stubble as it tugged at the fabric of her glove.

Without hesitation, he pulled her in, meeting her mouth in a kiss that was as intense as it was powerful. Strong arms enveloped her, drawing her into the lee of his commanding presence. His kiss demanded she return the passion, and, without a thought, she kissed him back, instinctively. His flavor was familiar and igniting, comforting and compelling all at once. The soft scent of the orange grove swirled around her, adding to the magic of the moment. His teeth tugged at her lower lip as he pressed against her, reminding her of the power in his arms. Reaching up, she allowed her fingers the delight of exploring the planes and ridges of his shoulders, adding to the attraction already smoldering within.

His fingers traced up her arms, teasing the ribbon at her neckline then lacing behind her head as if removing himself from a sweet temptation. His kiss gentled as he continued to playfully nip at her lips. Beatrix held him close, losing herself in the moment, committing every nuance to memory as she traced his lower lip with her tongue as he lingered.

"Come away with me," he whispered against her mouth.

"No," she replied, nipping his lip impishly. Surely he hadn't asked in earnest.

He pulled her in tighter with a slightly irritated growl before he lowered his head to trail kisses down her neck. "Yes."

"No... you're mad." Beatrix spoke far too breathlessly to be taken seriously.

His tongue tickled her neck as he whispered, "I prefer persuasive."

"I'd say incessant," she shot back as she leaned away to meet his gaze.

He grinned then reached up to tug on a curl that had fallen near her face. "Incessantly persuasive."

"Fair... but you must know that I cannot go anywhere with you. I'm here with Lady Southridge, and I cannot leave."

"Why?" His grin faded. "It is all but apparent that you were not abducted, as I was led to believe, and, according to my deductions from reason, it is only logical that the duke was at least somehow aware that Lady Southridge took you away. Dear heavens..." He took a step back. "...please tell me she has not deluded herself into thinking she's your protection!"

"I have no idea to what you are referring—"

"You indeed do, so do not insult my intelligence with so weak a lie." He spoke in clipped tones.

Beatrix folded her hands in front of herself and stepped away. "I'm afraid I cannot give to you that which you ask."

"Then I'm afraid I have no other option," Lord Neville replied and started toward her.

"Wh-what do you think you're doing?" Beatrix asked, not sure how to interpret the determined gleam in his eye.

"What I should have done in the library months ago," he mumbled.

Beatrix backed up till she felt the cool stone wall at her back. At his knowing grin, she narrowed her eyes and turned to run.

But he was too quick. In one motion, he swept her into his arms and proceeded to walk toward the orangery's exit.

"What are you doing?" Beatrix demanded as she struggled in his arms. One foot was able to get a proper kick to his person, and he grunted in response.

"Miss Lamont, I'll be quite upset if you ruin this jacket," he replied with far too much control.

Irritated by his composed attitude, Beatrix gave another kick just to spite him.

"You'll pay for that later," he promised.

"We shall see about that. Now, let me down! I demand it!" she shrieked as she bucked in his arms again. "What exactly are you planning to do? Waltz up to Breckridge House and knock on the door?"

"Waltzing would prove to be difficult at this point… however, walking up to the front door will suffice."

"Why?"

"I believe that was *my* question… to which you fully refused to answer… therefore requiring me to resort to my more assertive measures."

"This is not assertive. This is asinine!" Beatrix glared then gasped as she had a brilliant idea. Without hesitation, she reached up and mussed his hair, causing the dark chocolate curls to go from tame to wild as they erratically stuck from his head.

"What—? Did you truly—?" He all but dropped her and ran his fingers through his hair.

Beatrix wasted no time and sprinted as fast as her slippered feet could carry her across the grass toward Breckridge House.

The sound of Lord Neville pursuing her was enough incentive to give one final burst of speed that would have surely gotten her to the safety of the servants' entrance, if not for the root of a tree that seemed to spring out of the earth. One moment she was running, cursing her corset as she gasped for breath; the next moment she was flat on her back, unable to breathe at all. Hands at her throat, she tried to gasp, but no air entered her starving lungs.

"Damn it all," Lord Neville swore then hauled her up and, with one hand, felt for the laces of her corset.

And the world faded to grey.

NEVILLE GROUND OUT A low oath as he felt the hoyden in his arms go limp. To be honest, in his efforts to restrain her, he hadn't acted in the most gentlemanly fashion, but that was the way it was with Miss Lamont. He lost his bloody mind around her; all rational thought evaporated like water on a hot stone. He felt for the offending corset then reached down and withdrew a knife from his boot. With one motion, he carefully slid the knife's edge along the back of her gown, damning himself with each snap of the laces, till the garment hung loosely, exposing the creamy white skin at her back. Glancing away from the temptation, he laid her gently on her back, taking a deep breath when he noticed the soft rise and fall of her chest, signifying the life-giving intake of oxygen. It was hard enough to get the breath knocked out of oneself, let alone while wearing a corset.

Another reason to thank the good Lord he was a man.

Though he had to give her credit for the speed at which she ran; it was impressive to gain that kind of velocity in skirts.

He studied her face, tempted to count the smattering of freckles on her nose, the kind that simply highlighted the softness of her skin. They were a reflection of the caramel tones of her eyes; eyes that were just starting to flutter open. Long lashes blinked as her gaze grew in focus. Damn, but she was beautiful. It was no wonder he lost all reason around her. But it wasn't her outer beauty that has so captivated him… it was her wit, her inability to take him seriously.

Ever since the incident with Mary — heavens above, how

he wanted to forget it all — everyone in the *ton* had done one of two things: feared him or ignored him. Neither of which were boons as far he was concerned. But Miss Lamont, *Beatrix,* as he thought of her… When everyone else had given him a wide berth, she'd elbowed him in the ribs; when everyone else had deferred to him, she'd put him in his place. In the library at Greenford Waters, it had taken him all but a few seconds to know she was different, that she was, in a word, perfect — for him at least.

But, of course that hadn't given him license to kiss her like he had, regardless of how much he'd wanted to continue kissing her… amongst other things. But that was before, when he'd assumed he'd have time to pay her court, to clear the mystery surrounding his name before approaching the duke with his suit for her hand. Then she had been taken, or so he'd thought, and all the other details had seemed trivial.

So here he stood — sat, rather — in the middle of the English countryside with Miss Beatrix flat on her back, gasping as she filled her lungs with air and completely unlaced… without one ounce of pleasure to be had by either of them! How was it possible? Irony at its best. He could do nothing but laugh as he considered the situation.

"Why, in heaven's name, are you laughing?" she ground out between breaths. Her brown eyes were stormy and angry, yet all he felt was a deepening of his attraction, a delight at finding some new nuance about her.

"It is of no consequence," he replied, choking back his mirth as he stood.

"I doubt that," she said a bit easier since her breath was now less labored. She made a movement to sit up, her eyes widening like tea saucers as she reached back to feel her, well… back.

"You— How—? I cannot believe—"

"I assure you it was all in efforts to save your life, not ravish you… though I must say the idea does have some merit—"

Her growl cut off his words.

"If I could stand, I'd slap that grin right off your handsome face.

"Oh, so you think I'm handsome? I always fancied I was quite dashing in grey."

"I loathe you."

"Ah, I'm quite fond of you myself." He shrugged. "But considering your current state of well… undress, I do think we ought find you a way to remain decent. Wouldn't want to offend my tender gentlemanly sensibilities."

"You are impossible."

"Not entirely."

"Yes, entirely, completely and unequivocally." She lay back down and closed her eyes. "What exactly happened to me?"

He glanced up as a few servants exited the nearby door and gasped as they saw them then rushed back inside. By his estimation, he had about two minutes before Lady Southridge found them. Which would play into his plan quite nicely… better than his original plan in fact.

He took a seat beside Beatrix and patted her hand patronizingly, loving the leap of annoyance in her expression as he did so. "You were overwhelmed with my kissing prowess and fainted in my arms. But don't worry…" He leaned in. "…your secret is safe with me."

"Liar… I distinctly remember running *from* you."

"Odd." He shrugged.

"And tripping…"

"You are quite clumsy," he added with a grin.

"Am not! Of all my sisters, I'm the most graceful," she replied with a pout.

"Not high praise for your sisters, I'm afraid." He tugged at his cravat. Surely, the neck cloth was beyond repair, so he tugged at the offense and removed it completely.

It would add to the story.

"Do not do that! You can't just remove your neck cloth!" Beatrix scolded in a whisper as she glanced about from her position on her back. "No, no — this won't do. I must— You must— Turn around!" she demanded as she sat up, holding the back of her dress together as she did so.

"Why can I not remove it? After all, I'm still far more presentable than you, my dear," he shot back as he stood and reached out to help her stand. "Are you stable?" he asked gently as she placed all her weight on her feet.

"Yes, no thanks to you," she spoke with derision.

"I do believe I saved your life. A little more gratitude would be appreciated."

"For the last time, I was running *from* you! You are the reason I'm even in this state!" She took a tentative step and then hissed.

"You're injured. Let me help." He reached for her.

"No, you have helped quite enough," she bit out and backed away, but her ankle must have been weakened from the fall, and she began to stumble.

Lord Neville reached out, grasped her waist, and pulled her in, supporting her. His gloved hands touched the soft skin of her exposed back. Bloody gloves, always in the way! Lilac and rose clung to her skin, and he inhaled deeply, committing the scent to memory. What had started in the library many months ago was about to be finished in only a few seconds, if he had any say in it.

Then, better than he could have ever orchestrated it, Lady Southridge burst through the servants' entrance, three footmen with her. Her eyes grew wide, then her red eyebrows lowered as he saw her gaze dart between him and the lady in his arms…surely taking in their disheveled state.

"Leave me," she commanded, and the three footmen scattered.

Even Neville was slightly nervous due to the edge in her

tone.

Beatrix's eyes widened then closed as Lady Southridge spoke. Her soft shoulders slumped, and she cast a pleading gaze to him, which pierced his heart, but then the expression changed to one of absolute outrage.

Lady Southridge took a few determined strides toward them then paused. "Beatrix, are you well?" she asked.

Her tone betrayed her concern, and Neville had a pang of regret, but it was short-lived. Truly, this was for the best.

They might not see it now, but surely they'd see it eventually.

They had to.

"Yes. I'm as well as can be expected after being accosted, carried, and bested by a tree root," she replied as she glanced over her shoulder.

"Accosted?" Lady Southridge asked, her gaze raking the back of Beatrix's gown. "I do believe this is a conversation which should take place inside. Come."

"Lady Southridge—" he started, only to be interrupted by Beatrix.

"Wait, not like that…" Beatrix turned to face Lady Southridge. "He accosted me but not… like that."

He glanced down, and, sure enough, she was tapping her fingers against her thumb once again.

He smiled to himself, loving that he knew something so trivial about her. Because, in his opinion, it was the trivial things that added up to large, important things. It was the trivial things that had ended up destroying Mary… destroying him.

"Very well, we still must address… this," Lady Southridge spoke, her tone concerned.

Beatrix nodded and started to take a step toward the door, limping in her effort.

*In for a penny, in for a pound.* Without delay, Lord Neville swept her into his arms once more, careful to keep her dress at least somewhat intact at her back, and strode to the door with a very silent Beatrix in his arms. He did his best to ignore the evil glare from Lady Southridge.

"You have some explaining to do, young man," she murmured as they entered the heavy wooden entrance.

He met her scowl. "As do you, my lady."

# CHAPTER FOUR

BEATRIX WAS SURE SHE WAS AFLAME with the burn of humiliation that stung her cheeks and sizzled in her chest. How *dare* he! To think she had dreamed of being kissed by him once again, only to discover that the gentleman she'd once imagined him to be was all a lie. Barnyard pigs had more manners… and she had seen peacocks less arrogant. Yet, even as the anger burned within her, she still wasn't able to ignore the soft intake of breath that caused his chest to rise and fall as she leaned against it while they passed through the old stone servant's entrance and proceeded to climb the creaking stairs. The wooden door that allowed entrance to the main floor loomed ahead, noiselessly opening as Lady Southridge twisted the old brass knob. Even as all this happened around her, she couldn't quite pull her attention from the man holding her. The scent of cinnamon and peppermint clung to his skin and called to her, reminding her of the flavor of his kiss, the warmth of his embrace.

Damn the man.

How could someone infuriate her so fully and yet captivate her senses so utterly? It was entirely unfair.

Regardless of how he affected her, the last thing she was going to allow was for him to be aware! She'd rather rot.

"I do believe this is the most silence I've ever experienced in your company," he murmured to her.

Lady Southridge turned slightly and gave him a piercing glare.

The maddening man simply winked at her.

Had he *no* shame? Had he no idea what was ahead of them? Of what their situation implied?

Dear heavens.

*She* didn't even want to think about what their situation inferred.

And here he was, winking at the woman completely capable and within her right to demand he marry Beatrix!

He had to be mad, fully and completely mad.

Beatrix turned her head to fully study him. His walnut-brown hair was still in a scattered array from her earlier attempt to escape his arms, yet, mussed as it was, it was more becoming than his perfectly combed style. It added a hint of playfulness otherwise hidden. His full lips twisted wryly as he regarded her study of his person. "Don't worry, this is not the first time I've stunned a lady into silence from simply being in my arms. I can promise a full recovery," he remarked, a teasing tone to his voice.

Unable to restrain herself, Beatrix reached up and smacked the back of his head.

"I do believe that was uncalled for." Neville shook his head scoldingly, and readjusted her in his arms. In the process, her ruined dress exposed the flesh in her back fully.

Gasping, she struggled to right herself but was unable to fight his strength. "I'd play nicely," he whispered quietly, a mischievous gleam in his eye. "Why were you studying me?" he asked, as if sensing the need to distract her from causing him bodily harm.

The man was smarter than he let on.

"I was trying to determine if one could tell you were utterly mad simply by looking at you," Beatrix ground out.

"Lovely. I find I'm utterly riveted on the findings of your research." His tone was dry and amused.

Beatrix all but growled. "I find I can't make a rational conclusion due to the immense amount of anger I have toward you right now."

"Ah, Bea, you don't mean that."

"Bea? No. I *hate* that name," Beatrix replied hotly.

"Why? I think it's quite perfect." He shrugged as much as possible while holding a fully-grown woman in his arms.

They neared the parlor door, and Beatrix struggled to keep her anxiety in check.

"I don't care what you think. I dislike it." She spoke distractedly as they entered the red parlor, and Lady Southridge gestured to a chair for him to place her.

Gently, far more than she would have expected, he lowered her into the soft brocaded chair. Without a word, he located a small cushioned stool and lifted her leg ever so cautiously till it was resting atop of it.

Careful to not move more than necessary, Beatrix was relieved to feel no additional pain. Though it wasn't proper for him to even mention her ankle, let alone touch it, she couldn't help but be stirred by the sensitivity by which he took care of her.

"I do think that is quite enough," Lady Southridge huffed as she inclined her head toward a chair far away from Beatrix.

Neville glanced to Beatrix, and, though the eye contact was brief, she could clearly see his amusement. Obediently, he took a seat and reclined enough to be proper, yet it was evident in his posture that nothing about the situation caused him distress.

The man had to be cracked. Did he honestly believe his actions would have no consequence?

Astounded, Beatrix could only flick her gaze between

Lady Southridge and Lord Neville, waiting for someone to throw the gauntlet.

"Lady Southridge, you have *not* been forthright," he began, dusting his trousers absently.

"Lord Neville—" Lady Southridge started, her tone anything but passive.

He lifted his hand as if commanding her to stop.

And to Beatrix's great surprise, Lady Southridge paused.

Why, that was akin to parting the Red Sea! Just what was afoot?

"You had me under the impression that your lady's companion was an aged widow... not the vibrant beauty before us." He stood and walked to the back of his chair and rested his hands upon it.

"Pardon?" Beatrix asked before she could think better of it.

"Why, I do believe you *laughed* when I mentioned the stable boy at Fox Inn had described your lady's companion, Bev, a beauty," he stated, lowering his chin and giving a direct gaze at Lady Southridge.

Completely at a loss as to what was going on, Beatrix turned her gaze to the older woman, wondering if she shared her confusion.

Lady Southridge's eyes narrowed at the man, then she nodded ever so slightly. Adjusting her skirt slightly, she shifted. "You understand I need to protect my interests. How very inconvenient for me, should I hire a lady's companion I actually enjoy, only to have her snatched from my service by some gentleman in search of a wife? No. You must understand my predicament."

"But—" Beatrix tried to interject.

"I do understand, Lady Southridge, but the deception..." Neville interrupted Beatrix then took a few lazy steps to the left of the chair and faced Lady Southridge fully, his gaze direct and intent. "...but your deception was foolhardy. How can you expect to protect your... interests... so improperly prepared, should the worst happen? I must say… your young lady's companion would have been easy prey had I not been a gentleman."

Beatrix cast him a disbelieving look. His interpretation of *gentleman* must be much looser than that of hers.

"I can see the folly of my ways. However…" Lady Southridge stood. "…there is the matter of your behavior, Lord Neville, toward someone of my employ. An unmarried woman at that." She tilted her head slightly.

"I am present… just in case you had forgotten that detail," Beatrix spoke in an annoyed tone, lamenting her injury that prevented her from standing as well. "And both of you have lost your wits! Everyone in this room already knows that—"

"Miss — Bev, I would suggest you cease speaking, or else I'll be forced to kiss you once more, stunning you into silence again." He gave her a wink.

Beatrix felt her face heat with anger and humiliation once more. Was it possible to be in the same room with that man and not feel so emotionally engaged? She either wanted to kiss him or kill him.

Neither were wise ideas.

"So you've kissed her?" Lady Southridge asked, walking in a loose circle around him, like a lioness circling her prey.

Beatrix swallowed hard against what she knew was coming. Unable to decide how she felt about it, she simply stared as Lady Southridge measured up the man before her.

Lord Neville didn't flinch, but met her gaze directly, as if daring her to continue.

As if it were part of the plan.

*Heavens above! The man has planned this!*

"No. No, no, no, you did *not!*" Beatrix narrowed her eyes and tried to stand, but rather flopped back into the chair in a decidedly ungraceful motion. Glaring at him, she spat. "How could you!? *Why* would you? You do not know me!"

"I know you well enough to know what I'm doing. Please

calm yourself."

She gasped. *Calm* herself? As if this was simply a walk in Hyde Park!

"Bev, it would seem that Lord Neville just admitted to taking liberties with you. Now, I must ask… Were these liberties welcomed?" Lady Southridge queried, and Beatrix felt the color drain from her face.

Turning to face her, Beatrix swallowed. It would be so easy to lie… to say it had been unwanted attention… forced even.

But lying had never been an option for her. To speak so fully in opposition to the truth went against everything within her. So, knowing she was sealing her fate, she simply nodded and closed her eyes so she'd not see the disappointment on Lady Southridge's face.

"Then I believe we have a wedding to plan."

Beatrix had expected the words to be spoken in a dull, lifeless tone. But she'd been mistaken.

Opening her eyes, she saw Lady Southridge's grin, wide and free as she winked at her.

Winked.

As if she hadn't just been compromised.

By the very man from which they were trying to get riddance!

A pulsing throb began at the back of her neck. The world must have somehow turned on its ear!

And why were they insisting on calling her Bev? Had they all lost their bloody minds? It was the parlor! It wasn't as if they needed to keep with the ruse… unless…

"Brilliant," Lord Neville replied and bowed. "If you'll excuse me, I have some affairs to attend to at present, given the recent circumstances. By your leave."

"Of course, but you will be back to take dinner with us, will you not?" Lady Southridge asked, rather than demanded.

Beatrix glanced between them, trying to pull the pieces of

the scattered puzzle together in her mind.

"Of course. Lady Southridge, you must know, I will not be far, should… Bev… need me." There was a weight to his words, as if trying to convey some secretive meaning.

"Very good." She nodded.

Lord Neville strode toward Beatrix, his gaze dark and inviting, as if being rewarded, rather than punished, for his bad behavior. His expression was fascinating, and she steeled herself against it, knowing there was far more going on than met the eye.

And she vowed to find it out.

"Miss… Bev," he spoke softly then reached for her hand and kissed it tenderly. "I must say that the day has taken a delightful turn. I do hope you'll come to the same conclusion soon," he whispered then quit the room, leaving the scent of cloves in his wake.

"Well, I couldn't have planned that better." Lady Southridge clapped her hands once his footsteps were out of earshot.

"Pardon?" Beatrix glared at her, careful to hold her dress together in the back.

"My dear, for being so intelligent, you really miss the obvious, don't you?" She clicked her tongue. "You are the safest you could possible be! Wedded to Lord Neville? Why—? Wait! You don't know who he is, do you?" Lady Southridge paused as apparent understanding dawned across her face.

"He's a previously reclusive lord who decided to re-enter society and be the bane of my existence," Beatrix replied hotly.

Shaking her head, Lady Southridge spoke. "My dear, you may try to fool yourself, but no one else believes that lie about your indifference to him. The very air about you heats when you two are together. It was the same at the library in Greenford Waters."

"How—?"

"I have my ways. Now… it's not my story to tell. But I do

believe you should speak with your future husband tonight after dinner. His past is one that will lend security but, potentially, fear. You alone can make that decision." She walked to the door. "Now I suggest we get you properly attired. After all, you have a betrothed to impress at dinner."

NEVILLE SIGNED HIS NAME with a flourish and closed the envelope with the warm wax before pressing his seal atop. The Neville crest imprinted perfectly, an impressive and bold *N* with a shield behind it. Distinctive yet elegant. He glanced about the rented room at the Goose Inn and collected his belongings. The room was unused, save the necessity of the desk, as his plan had worked out far better than he'd imagined.

Betrothed.

He dared not consider the full implications lest he become far too distracted by the truth of it… the pleasure to be had. But there were far more pressing matters needing his full attention. That Beatrix had not caught on when he and Lady Southridge had continued to call her Bev, even within the Breckridge House walls, was a situation he'd have to address with her forthwith. No one could be trusted, no risks taken. Lady Southridge had immediately caught on to his plan; that much was evident. At times, he didn't know how to read the woman; rather, she was oblivious in some matters, or simply wanted others to perceive her as such, so that she might uncover deeper secrets. If so, the woman would be quite the asset to the crown, not that he'd ever mention that.

Bloody hell, he could only imagine what would happen should she feel the need to serve her country!

He swiped the sealed letters from the desk and tucked them into his front coat pocket. He'd have them delivered by messenger immediately. Of course, it would cause quite the gush of gossip within the *ton*, but that was the point.

Draw them out…

So that the shadows could no longer hide their intentions.

And once they were exposed, he'd eliminate the threat.

It was a tried and true method. Simple yet effective.

And as long as he could keep the ruse of Bev going, Beatrix would be completely safe.

Just thinking her name made his body respond. It was stronger than before, the siren call she held over him. It was as if every kiss, every touch only made him crave more. He chuckled. She would keep his life interesting that was for certain. Beatrix was no simpering deb.

He settled with the inn and strode outside to his mount. It was delightful to travel so light, to be able to bypass the necessity of a carriage. Though it was rare for a man of his title to do so, he found it refreshing to simply blend in. The members of the *ton* usually wished to stand out, but he had never been comfortable doing so. And when his life had gone to hell, he'd found sanctuary in the solitude of isolation. Everything around him seemed to remind him of Mary, of her betrayal and of the blood on his hands.

From that choice to remain in self-imposed exile, he had been astounded at how the rumors had grown. And he had let them… encouraged them even. Because the more horrendous they'd become, the more the *ton* had left him alone.

Let him lick his wounds.

And he would have been quite satisfied to remain in that sorry state had he not received the missive from the war office.

A man with nothing to lose didn't fear death.

So, with reckless abandon, he'd thrown himself into the job. At first they had only requested his assistance with intelligence, but when he'd proven himself, they'd allowed him to take a smaller case. From there, his reputation had simply grown.

Till last season when they'd had a need for him to

immerse himself in society once more.

He still remembered the cold chill of understanding as his superior had given him the assignment. It had been a strange awakening to not fear the most deadly of criminal, yet feel a cold sweat break out when thinking about attending a ball.

It was that realization that had made him determined to accept the assignment. Fear would not hold such power over him…

*He decided to attend the come out of a debutant, one who would surely pull in all of London's elite to one event: the ward of a duke. Bethanny Lamont's come out was sure to be a smashing success, and he was attending.*

*But it wasn't the incomparable nature of her debut that captivated his attention.*

*No, it was a dark-haired beauty that seemed to be sneaking in, watching from atop a balcony overlooking the large ballroom. It was easy to deduce that it was a sister of the debutant of the evening, given their similar appearance. Later, he found out her name: Beatrix.*

*And from that moment, he subtly uncovered more and more about her, about her family.*

*Because in the* ton, *nothing was what it seemed.*

*Ever.*

*But just because it was deceptive, didn't mean it needed to be brought to light.*

*No, some secrets were meant to remain hidden.*

*And that was exactly what Neville had been trying to do, till the wrong person used them against the very girl who captivated him.*

*He was rather proud of his self-control; that was, until a secluded afternoon in the library of Greenford Waters…*

But that was now history.

Delicious, decadent, and enticing history that was bound to be a very prominent part of his future.

He urged his mount into a gallop down the well-worn road toward Breckridge House. The post he'd left with the innkeeper, to be sent out immediately, would start the plan in motion. Protecting Beatrix, yet setting a trap at the same time, pulling the hidden nemesis out into the light.

With the simple task completed, he set out to apply himself to the more trying, yet infinitely more pleasurable undertaking of winning his soon-to-be-wife's heart.

# CHAPTER FIVE

BEATRIX STRUGGLED TO REMAIN COMPOSED as she descended the stairs. She wasn't quite sure which emotion was creating such havoc within her: irritation or attraction.

Odd how the two emotions seemed to be in constant conflict whenever she was in the company of the reclusive Lord Neville.

Her betrothed.

Honestly, just how had she gotten herself into such a position?

She snorted indelicately as she remembered that it wasn't her own actions, rather his, that had found them in such an arrangement.

Irritation won for a moment. Yet as she walked across the foyer toward the parlor where they'd meet before heading to supper, her heart skipped while she took in the dark gaze of Lord Neville as he stood in acknowledgment of her entrance. His charcoal coat accentuated his dark features, but rather than the contrast making him appear severe, it only highlighted his strong jaw, the intelligent wit and appreciation flashing in his deep brown eyes.

"Miss Bev." He bowed.

A snort escaped her lips unchecked, and she blushed as she realized her blunder.

He met her gaze with an amused grin.

She squared her shoulders. "Must we—?"

"Certainly your lady will be down shortly?" he interrupted, his dark brows lowering as if conveying some message.

She paused. "Yes, of course." Beatrix took a deep breath and walked over to the fireplace. She watched the orange flames hungrily lick the wood.

"Surely you must understand the need for us to maintain appearances… Bev." His words were hot in her ear.

She jumped slightly at the sound of his voice, not having heard his approach.

"Why?" she asked, inhaling deeply the rich scent of him.

"Because we are not certain who is friend, who is foe," he whispered, his breath tickling her neck.

"I highly doubt that—"

"I'd rather not risk this beautiful neck of yours," he murmured as he ran a finger along it. Immediately her skin burst into goose bumps, and she quite forgot whatever thought she'd been considering.

"Such lovely skin."

"Th-thank you," Beatrix replied, unable to manage more as the man was creating the most wicked desire swirling within her, all with a simple touch.

The man was either antagonizing her or seducing her.

She rather liked the seducing part.

"Lady Southridge has created quite a clever cover for you. We shall exploit it to the best of our ability. It shall give us extra aid in protecting you."

"Us?" Beatrix asked, her mind snapping alert.

"I quite imagine that we agree on the priority of keeping you safe, along with Lady Southridge. However…" He paused and placed a soft kiss to her neck just where her shoulder began. "I wouldn't hesitate to take on the task alone."

She inhaled a shaky breath. "Why?" she managed.

"Why not?" he replied as his fingers traced her jawline.

"I do believe you understood my question. After all, we haven't known each other long. I'll not enter into an arrangement with you—"

"An engagement… not arrangement," he corrected.

"Very well, an engagement with you… on so weak a foundation of the small knowledge we have of one another," she finished, turning from the fire and stepping away so that she might face him without his provocative touch assaulting her senses.

"What makes you think I know so little about you?" he asked, hitching a shoulder slightly.

Her brow furrowed, and he chuckled.

"I do know more about you than you think, sweet Bev, but even if I did not, there are many marriages of the *ton* that are based upon far less."

"Be that as it may…" She clasped her hands in front of her. "…I refuse to add myself to their ranks."

"Nor would I expect you to." He took a small step toward her. "I would hate to sentence myself to such a fate either."

His advance toward her continued till he was close enough for her to see the slight silk pattern in his cravat. The small swirling design captivated her — rather provided the distraction from his alluring presence that she needed in order to keep her wits about her.

"Look at me," he demanded in a seductive whisper.

"No," she replied, yet glanced up.

"Yes."

"I do believe you enjoy arguing with me." He placed a finger under her chin, holding her gaze.

"I do believe you delight in provoking me," she retorted.

Undeterred by her barb, he simply chuckled. "Possibly."

He studied her mouth, his gaze smoldering as he slowly leaned down.

Beatrix closed her eyes and waited, fully anticipating the kiss, knowing she should be doing anything but appearing so eager.

But she couldn't quite muster the denial of the truth.

As much as she loathed the man… she also quite liked him far too much to deny her attraction or the pleasure of his kiss.

The moment his lips touched hers, the sound of footsteps assaulted her senses as equally as his warmth.

"That is enough, you two. I will not have my lady's maid compromised in the parlor." Lady Southridge's voice spoke calmly, as if she were commenting on the weather.

Beatrix stepped back, heat flushing her face as she bumped into a chair and knocked it over.

"Don't get into such a dither, Bev. It's not the first time he's kissed you," Lady Southridge commented. "Am I not correct, Lord Neville?"

"Indeed you are correct, my lady." He bowed, the traitor.

Beatrix took a calming breath and tried to regain her composure. She glanced to the offending chair, still on its side, and then narrowed her eyes at Lord Neville.

"Well, it's not," he defended, though a smirk broke through his innocent expression. He strode to the upended piece of furniture and righted it.

"Bev, do come and sit by me," Lady Southridge all but commanded.

Beatrix glared daggers at Lord Neville but obeyed. Her skirts swished lightly as she crossed the parlor floor and took a seat beside the dowager.

"You may also sit, Lord Neville… if you wish," Lady Southridge added after patting Beatrix's shoulder.

"I'll stand, if you don't mind."

"I rather thought you'd do so," Lady Southridge replied.

The conversation stalled, the crackling of the fire the only sound in the room. Finally, Lady Southridge broke the silence. "Were you able to accomplish all that was necessary this afternoon? I gather you'll be reoccupying your rooms here at Breckridge House?"

"Indeed," Lord Neville replied and took a casual step toward Lady Southridge. "Surely my presence is more…welcome than before?" He smirked then glanced to the fire as if trying to hide his amusement.

"That is still up for debate, young man." Lady Southridge replied with a dry tone.

Beatrix glanced heavenward, searching her mind for some intelligent remark that would break up the awkward moment.

"Of course…my favor could be earned." Lady Southridge studied her gloves, then glanced meaningfully to Lord Neville.

"Anything for you, my lady."

Lady Southridge snorted. "Is that so? Well, then I'll look forward to a quiet evening to myself after we dine. It would seem you have much to discuss with Bev. Much that has been…left undisclosed." She leaned forward slightly.

"I see." Lord Neville nodded. "Then I shall anticipate a few moments of privacy with Bev, by your leave of course."

Beatrix's gaze danced from Lord Neville, then back to Lady Southridge as if following a tennis ball being lobbed from one opponent to another. Taking a deep breath she stood, thankful her ankle had improved so quickly. "I'm quite certain Lord Neville will disclose all that is necessary, Lady Southridge. And," She turned her attention to Lord Neville. "I'm also positive that Lady Southridge will provide us with the necessary privacy to conduct such a necessary conversation." She folded her hands in front of herself, careful not to tap her fingers, as she was sorely tempted to do.

As if reading her thoughts Lord Neville's glance darted to her hands and then back, a knowing grin teasing his lips.

Drat the man!

"Since that is all settled, I do believe the meal is ready."

Lady Southridge stood and tilting her head, extended her hand in invitation for Lord Neville's escort.

"At your service." Lord Neville led her from the room, but not before he glanced back and winked at Beatrix as she moved to follow their lead.

Shaking her head, all she could think was that she surely hoped dinner was less eventful. She'd need the peaceful moments to prepare for what would surely be an intense conversation afterward.

A conversation she was both anticipating, yet dreading.

AFTER DINNER LORD NEVILLE found himself in a cozy parlor with the most tempting woman he'd ever met. And as fate would have it, he had to lay bare all the danger that lay before them, as well as the past that haunted him still. So with a tight chest, he tried to convey as much as possible, without adding to the fear he saw haunting her gaze. "I understand that it is quite difficult to comprehend all this information at once," He finished.

Beatrix needed time to think, to process all that he had so recently laid bare. Truthfully, he didn't trust himself at the moment either. Never before had he felt so vulnerable, so exposed. Normally he couldn't care a fig what others thought of him.

But he did care what she thought.

He found that he cared quite bit.

Which was why he found himself holding his breath before forcing himself to breathe evenly as he waited for her reaction. Her face was impassive, but it was her eyes that gave away her emotions.

And heaven bless Lady Southridge for giving them some semblance of privacy. He'd have to thank her later. A door slightly ajar was not a common blessing, but he'd use it to his full advantage. Dinner had proven quite relaxing, but as it had wound to an end, he'd known the necessity of having a private conversation with Beatrix.

"I understand… most of it. Rather, I find I'm quite confused on only one aspect." Her body was slightly tilted toward the fire so that the firelight flickered across her features, causing her skin to glint with light.

He swallowed hard, tried to focus on her words.

But found he was quite incapable.

He had always prided himself on his ability to keep a cool head, to think through even the most precarious situations, yet he found himself completely unable to do so with her in the room.

"What aspect?" he asked, his tone betraying his arousal.

She flushed and glanced away. "I hardly think this is the time to—"

"Rather, I believe it is the perfect time." Neville spoke quickly and strode toward her, keeping his approach purposeful, yet still cautious. It seemed as if he had been rather boorish with her of late; the last thing he wanted her to think was that her future husband was a brute.

No, she deserved wooing, romance, and the like.

And there was no time like the present.

Holding out his hand, he waited.

She glanced from his hand to his eyes then back, a question in her gaze.

He wiggled his fingers.

"You have no gloves on." she reminded him, her tone dubious.

He gasped and placed his other hand to his mouth to hide his teasingly shocked expression. "I promise you my bare skin is quite clean."

She shot him an irritated expression.

Just to harass her further, he studied his extended hand momentarily. "Yes, free of any dirt. I promise not to ruin your lovely dress."

"It's not my dress I'm afraid of ruining," Beatrix shot back, but he could see the indecision fading from her eyes.

He was learning something fascinating. As much as he was drawn to her, unable to deny her siren call, she was drawn equally to him.

Bloody hell, that was as addictive as it was terrifying.

He swallowed and held out his hand once more, feeling as if he were doing so much more than offering her a hand.

He was presenting his heart.

Tentatively, she reached out and placed her hand in his.

Her gloved hand slid across his palm till his fingers tightened around her palm, and he pulled her close, taking a step toward her as well.

"One thing…" he whispered, slipping his other hand into their embraced grasp and tenderly tugging on each finger of her white glove till it loosened from her fingers. He removed it, tossed it aside, and then held out his palm as silent petition for her other hand.

Wordlessly, she offered it…he repeated the process. It was startlingly erotic, to take off a lady's gloves.

Not just any lady.

Beatrix… his lady.

His soon-to-be wife.

He grinned simply thinking the words.

Lifting her hand, he slid his bare fingers across her palm before interlocking her fingers with his, savoring the warm skin-on-skin melting together, fusing.

"So soft," he murmured. Releasing one hand, he reached around and placed his palm on her waist. It was the perfect size, fitting his large hand. Not as dainty as the other ladies he'd danced with, whose waist size had seemed unnaturally small. It was as if she were made for him, to fit perfectly. The scent of rose water and lilac surrounded him. Her brown eyes were bottomless, searching his. The same sensation of exposure slammed into him, yet, as disconcerting as it was, there was no fear.

With no music but the rhythmic pounding of his heart in his ears, he started to lead her in a waltz. Following, she stepped with him, graceful and light on her feet. It was a tragedy that he had never danced with her before, but to be honest, he had never had the opportunity. He'd like to think that had he been given the opportunity, he would have taken shameless advantage — in the best sense. The most appropriate sense.

"I've never waltzed without music," she commented, as if feeling the need to fill the silence.

He led her about the room, the sensual swirl of give and take, ebb and flow that the waltz created through its fluid steps.

"I find that hard to believe." He spoke as he pulled her in slightly, immediately warmed by her body heat.

"And why is that?" she asked, a saucy tilt to her full lips. They were the perfect plum color, inviting and sweet.

"You have sisters. I'm quite certain you practiced waltzing with them, and I'm assuming you didn't always have music."

She arched an eyebrow. "That is where you're mistaken," she said with a twist of her mouth, a shy grin breaking through. She bit her lip and glanced away momentarily.

"Oh?" He counted the small smattering of freckles on her nose, light and playful but adding a dimension of depth to her perfect face.

"Indeed. Berty always sang."

"Ah, then I was indeed incorrect." He nodded slightly, grinning as she met his gaze with a welcoming expression.

And, in that moment, he discovered another attribute to Beatrix that further stole his heart. She was fun.

When spoken aloud, it might not seem romantic, but, in the moment, it was. It was perfect. Like her.

"You truly must cease your assumptions. You cannot be

right as often as you'd like," she quipped, not resisting as he adjusted his hold to be slightly more near.

"Mortal wounds you inflict on my confidence, my lady," he teased. It was incredible how such an intimate moment could be so full of joy, so absent of abrasive tension, but rather thick with expectancy and hope.

It was the hope that transfixed him. How long had it been since he had sincerely felt that emotion?

"I have all confidence that you shall recover fully," she replied dryly, pulling him back into the conversation.

He slowed down their waltz and re-approached the topic they had drifted from, the topic that needed closure. As much as he hated it.

He hesitated, not wanting to break the spell that had woven so powerfully around them, but knowing he needed to find out the truth she sought. "You never answered my inquiry about what aspect of my explanation caused confusion."

"Well… I wasn't exactly given the opportunity to give voice to my thoughts. I do believe you felt the need to dance," she replied archly, her face flushing with a warming blush. He was standing close enough he could practically feel the heat.

Endearing, that.

"Indeed. And if I may be so bold—"

"When have you *not* been bold?" Beatrix interrupted with unrestrained laughter.

"Indeed." He chuckled darkly. "However… I was intending to compliment your grace while dancing. I had impugned the integrity of your claim earlier—"

She tilted her head in confusion.

"When you said you were the most graceful of your sisters."

"Ah, yes, well, I'm trying to forget your behavior earlier. It was not becoming of a gentleman." She straightened her shoulders and gave him a mock scowl.

"A thousand apologizes. I'm simply trying to amend my earlier assessment since it was so inaccurate. You are, indeed, very graceful."

"Thank you." She nodded, a grin breaking through. "I know."

"Humble too."

"Quite."

Unable to resist, he chuckled.

She smiled in response, then it faded, replaced by a slight frown. "I find I'm confused on the aspect of the motive. It seems the Lamont estate, or whatever inheritance we have received, is the motive for whomever it is who wishes to cause us harm. It is only my sisters and I who are the heirs. No other relatives are living. They had to do quite the stretch to connect us with the duke in the first place, because no one else shared any connection. In order for someone to contest our right to the estate, whether we be living or not, they'd have to be related. Do you see my confusion?"

"Indeed. Which is why we've been investigating your family's history. So far we've come up with little, which is why I need to ask you some questions, to see if we are missing some pertinent information concerning your family. But first, you must understand one thing, Miss Bev." He led her to the seating area beside the crackling fire.

"Must you call me that even when we are alone?" Beatrix lamented in a soft voice, even as her gaze darted around the room.

"Indeed. There is no precaution too much in order to provide you with the utmost protection. Which is the point I wish to make, Miss Bev…" Then, leaning forward, he whispered in her ear. "…my sweet Beatrix…" He straightened but not before watching her gaze soften at the sound of her name. "So long as I have breath in me, no harm will come to you. Back home, I have one of my finest colleagues watching your family as well. You are safe."

"Who is watching Berty and Bethanny?" she aske voice small.

"I've been told that the earl has hired several guards. However, we don't see Bethanny as much of a target. Right now, it seems that the target is you, my dear. Berty is being protected by one of my good friends, Curtis Sheppard. He's surely lamenting his station, but he's utterly trustworthy.

She nodded slightly, her expression still worried.

He waited till she sat, then, breaking the social protocol, he sat beside her.

To hell with it all.

"Did your family have any enemies? Were there any servants who seemed to be resentful?" he asked, studying her expression, full of concentration.

"Not that I'm aware. I do believe Bethanny would probably be able to offer you more information than I, since she was older when we lived there... when my parents passed." He noted the hitch in her tone, as if she still truly missed them.

His parents had passed as well, many years ago, but being like so many other of the *ton*, his parents had had the idea that children were to be neither seen nor heard. His memories of his mother and father were few and always tempered with mixed emotions of both hope and disappointment. When they passed, he'd indeed been sorrowful, but had not lamented their dying as deeply as Beatrix appeared to lament hers.

"I'll be sure to inquire with Bethanny. In the meantime, is there anything at all you can remember? Did your parents have any connections with others who might have interest in their remaining estate?" he asked.

She glanced upward, as if trying to recall the information they needed. "I remember my father refused to see someone... a gentleman... shortly before the carriage accident. I'm not sure of his name. The only reason I remember it is because it was during dinner, and my mother was always adamant that there would be no interruptions during mealtimes. For the footman to risk her wrath and approach my father during supper… it made an impression on me.

"I see." He shifted in his seat, facing her fully. "Do you remember what happened after the servant approached your father?"

She took a deep breath then exhaled slowly as she seemed to search her mind. "My father listened then turned quite red, apparently greatly vexed. He whispered something to the footman, and my mother coughed when she overheard, as if trying to hide her shock." She tilted her head. "My mother never could hide her emotions, that much I remember with all certainty."

"Did your father leave with the footman?"

"No. But I remember a commotion in the foyer. It was not too terribly far from the dining hall. My sisters and I glanced to each other, curious, but my father simply continued to eat his meal, as if nothing had happened at all. We took our cue from him and ignored the distraction, and soon, everything was normal again. We were sent to the nursery early that night," she finished, staring into the fire as if reliving the memories, not simply speaking of them.

"Was there any further talk of the gentleman or the circumstance?" This information was possibly the break they needed to find the person behind the threat. He tried to hide his interest, lest he distract her from any memory, any detail. Only heaven knew how important it might be.

"I don't believe so. The next day my father remained in his study, which was very common, and my mother went visiting a few of our tenants. The Millers, I believe. It was later that week that their carriage overturned, killing them both." Her tone was soft, as if speaking it too loud would make it happen again, make it more real.

"I'm… very sorry for your loss," Neville replied, feeling at odds as to how to comfort her.

"Thank you. It was years ago now… but when I speak of it … it seems much more recent, the wound fresher." She sniffled slightly then straightened, as if disgusted with her emotion.

"It must have been very comforting to have parents that you knew well." He mused as he watched a clear tear trail down her cheek and disappear under her jaw.

"It was… it truly was," she admitted, her tone thick. Taking a deep breath, she smiled bravely. "Here I am, dithering like a ninny, and I have no idea of your family history. Are your parents living?" She straightened and faced him. Her brown eyes were glassy, reflecting the firelight and utterly stunning. There was no calculating glint, no hint of falsehood, nothing but innocent inquiry.

He glanced down and reached for her hand. As he laced his fingers through hers, savoring the skin-on-skin contact, he took a deep breath. "I did not know my parents as well as you, and so when they passed, while I was saddened, it was not as defining a moment as it was for you and your sisters."

"Oh." She blinked. "I'm sorry to hear that."

"I'm afraid I know nothing different, so don't let it affect you." He shrugged.

"But… wasn't that difficult as a child? I — I cannot imagine not having my mother around to comfort me when I was young… to know my father's soothing voice when I was afraid." Her expression was pained as she glanced down then met his gaze once more, her eyes full of sympathy.

Brilliant.

"If you do not have something, you cannot miss its absence," he replied.

However, that wasn't the truth. Because he did miss those things she'd listed. But as a child, he hadn't been able to define them.

Not till he was older. And he vowed should he ever have his own heirs, they'd *know* him.

Not just his title or his name. They'd know *him*… the sound of his voice and the comfort of his affection.

"I suppose… though it still saddens me," she replied, reaching up and placing a warm hand to the side of his face.

"Don't waste your tears on the past." He leaned into her palm but kept his eyes trained on her.

Her pink tongue darted out and moistened her lips.

His body tightened, wanting, no, *needing* to further discover her flavor. Leaning forward, he waited, hoping she'd close the final distance, that she'd kiss *him.*

Her eyes closed, but she didn't move toward him. Indecisive, he watched her pink lips part slightly, but again, she didn't draw nearer.

Just as he was about to back away, her eyes opened and studied him with a confused expression. Holding his breath, he waited. Her warm breath tickled his lips, enticing him. A fraction of a moment before he damned his self-control and took her kiss, she leaned in, pressing her warm, inviting lips to his. The movement was so quick he didn't have a chance to close his eyes, but rather watched with rapt attention as she moved closer. Her kiss was tentative at first, then, as he returned it, he sensed her body relaxing into the movement, swaying into him. Eyes drifting close, he lost himself to the sensation of her freely given affection. She tasted of spicy tea and honey, his new favorite addiction.

She pulled away slightly, but he wasn't about to let her leave him. Biting her lip gently, he tugged her closer, enjoying her gasp of surprise that melted as he deepened the kiss. Her warm hand still framed his face, tightening as he ravaged her mouth, taking from her all the flavor he could consume. His hands wanted to be wicked, but he reigned in his own passion and settled for a possessive grasp on her shoulders coupled with feathered traces of his fingers down the side of her neck and arms, mapping her body, committing it to memory.

Heart pounding, he forced himself to remain a gentleman

when his mind was all too vividly reminding him how easily it would be to lean forward, inviting her to recline. From there, it would be so easy to—

No. Rather, he backed out of the kisses, feathering them till they came to an easy end.

When he opened his eyes, his focus narrowed on her swollen lips, pink and moist from his assault. Her eyes were a deep earthy brown, drunk with passion as her dark lashes accented their almond shape. In a word, she was breathtaking, rather — heart-taking.

"I really must stop allowing you such liberties." She spoke breathlessly, pressing two fingers to her lips, tracing them slightly.

Little did she know the gesture was like offering an invitation to a starving man.

Glancing away, he willed his desire under control.

"Have you ever considered that you're not allowing liberties as much as you're asking me for my freedom?" he asked, unable to glance away from her earnest gaze.

"Pardon?" she asked, her dark brows pinching in confusion.

He loosened his grip on her shoulders and trailed his fingers down her arms, pausing at her wrist. Then, taking a hand within both of his, he traced her fingers. "With every kiss, every touch, you seal my fate — my destiny. If I were truly taking liberties with you, I'd grow freer, rather than finding myself captured. Enraptured. Willingly," he whispered and glanced up. "And I found I'm quite content with the prospect."

She exhaled a shaky breath, as if his tender touch of her hand was just as powerful as his kiss.

He rather liked that idea.

"Either you are charming beyond compare, or you—" She glanced down, not finishing her sentence.

"Or I'm falling in love. It happens, you know. Your sister

is proof."

"Indeed, but I thought it happened — differently." She met his gaze, her heart in his eyes, but he could see the fear.

He recognized it because he felt it, the edge of it, bringing hard questions to his mind. But the risk it necessitated was nothing in comparison to the reward.

"I'm not the authority on the subject." He glanced away, knowing how accurate that statement was. "And I'm aware of the precarious risk in placing too much stock in emotion. We are English, are we not?" he teased, earning a slight smile.

"Indeed."

"But my affection is not dependent on my emotion. While love is what you feel, it is also what you choose. I choose you." He tilted up her chin, meeting her gaze.

"And you're certain of this decision?" The question was asked with the most direct gaze.

Rather than answer her, he placed a soft kiss to her lips. "Yes," he whispered, sealing his vow with another kiss, simply because he couldn't help himself.

After ending the kiss, he watched as her eyes fluttered open. "Although I do find myself doing quite a quantity of assurances to you… with little assurance from your end. A gentleman could easy become unsure in such a circumstance—"

His words were cut off with an eye roll followed by a fierce kiss that almost knocked him backward.

Not that he would have minded for her to be on top of him.

Rather, he lamented that he had stood firm; it would have been much more advantageous to allow her to knock him over.

Damn it all.

"That shall be your answer." She broke the kiss and nodded once.

"And what if I find I need further confirmation?" he

asked, knowing a wicked grin broke out across his face.

Smacking his shoulder, she shook her head good-naturedly. This was one of the many reasons he was falling so heavily for her. One moment they were passionately engaged in the most heated kisses; a moment later, they were joking, flirting — being friends.

It was enamoring, to have a friend — with such delightful benefits.

But more than a friend. A soulmate.

Was this what it was like?

No wonder other men made cakes of themselves!

His good friend, Curtis, would no doubt think he'd lost his bloody mind, if only he could see him now.

To hell with it all. He couldn't care a fig. One didn't question the gift of love, but simply took it and ran, protecting it with his life, till death did them part.

"You appear quite serious…" Beatrix traced his jawline with her fingers, bringing him back to the present.

"A thousand apologies." He reached up and grasped her hand, kissing it. "It has been quite the day," he murmured as he pressed her wrist to his mouth, kissing it again and then tracing the sensitive flesh of her wrist with his nose. "I do believe we should say goodnight… before I find myself tempted—"

"Understood." She pulled her wrist back, a deep blush staining her cheeks, though a secretive smile dashed across her features.

It was lovely, innocent, yet… not.

"I shall see you in the morning." He rose and extended his hand to help her stand.

Beatrix's hand met his, causing an undercurrent of desire to hum through him. He released her, against his will, and watched as she nodded then left. Pausing by the door, she turned, and with a slight wave, bit her lip and disappeared.

Expelling a large sigh, he sat back down and ran his

fingers though his hair. The woman would be the most dangerous distraction possible, one he both anticipated and also feared. He couldn't allow his guard down, not if he were to keep her safe. While he was quite certain their whereabouts were unknown, he didn't want to rely on that assumption.

In two days, he'd have word from Curtis, and the rest of the plan would be set in motion. In two days, he'd know what action to take.

Which was the easy part. The hard part? Convincing Beatrix.

His betrothed.

His love.

His addiction.

And quite possibly, the thorn in his side.

# CHAPTER SIX

BEATRIX BLINKED, HER EYES UNFOCUSED FROM the remnants of sleep. It had been two days since Lord Neville had practically accosted her. Signing, she snuggled farther into the warmth of the linen sheets and closed her eyes, a smile bending her lips as she thought about the past few days. Time had flown by, seeming to only have been marked by a glance, by a whisper or touch that made the fleeting moments stand still.

It was incredible how life could change so quickly.

Shifting so she could rise, she fisted her hands and stretched, placing her warm feet on the cool wooden floor.

As attentive as her betrothed had been, she sensed a tension underlying his smooth manner. Last night when she had approached the topic, she was relieved to discover her lover was more than willing to converse with her, not shutting her out as she had anticipated.

As warm as his embrace had been at the moment, her heart felt a sudden chill as she considered the reason for his tension. He had sent off a missive to London, to his friend Curtis Sheppard, and was awaiting word.

Blast the man, kind as he was, he was unwilling to divulge

any further information on the topic, other than, of course, what pertained to her.

As if that alleviated any curiosity!

Rather, it made it far worse!

He simply chuckled when she expressed her irritation.

Which only made her far more incensed!

Of course, that he'd decided to soothe her ruffled feathers with a heart-melting kiss only redeemed him slightly.

Very slightly.

But redeemed him nonetheless.

Beatrix sighed and shook her head. The man was far too charming for her good.

A knock sounded at the door, pulling her from her thoughts.

Her maid entered with a quick curtsey and, in short order, had Beatrix all properly attired for her role as Lady Southridge's companion.

Bah. She hated the need for playing the part, not that she objected to pretending to be a blue stocking — oddly that didn't bother her too greatly — it was that Lord Neville called her Bev.

She *hated* that.

Because when he spoke to her, it was her own name she wished to hear from his lips.

Not Bev.

Bev didn't exist, and, well… if she were being truly honest… that he called her Bev made her wonder if any of this were real.

Silly, foolish and insane, but it was the truth. She'd never claimed her emotions were rational.

What woman had?

Soon she was passing the richly wooden walls of Breckridge House. Light poured through large leaded-glass windows, making the house seem even larger than its massive size already boasted.

"Good morning," Lady Southridge called, her eyes not lifting from the newsprint before her. She sipped her tea gently and then replaced the cup to the matching saucer.

"Morning, ma'am." She curtseyed, falling into her practiced roll. Helping herself to a plate, she served herself. Crispy bacon and rich eggs with toast completed her meal, and she sat across from the dowager.

"I trust your night was well?" Beatrix offered kindly as she poured tea, watching the steam swirl from her cup.

"Passable." She lowered the newsprint, folded it, and picked up her tea with both hands.

Beatrix noted the date on the print, about a week ago, which was quite recent, considering how far into the country they were residing.

"Morning."

Lord Neville's voice melted over her like the butter on her warm toast. Her glance shot up to meet his, a shiver of delight vibrating along her heart. His dark eyes were rich and deep, like melted chocolate and just as delicious… and sinful.

"Morning to you as well, Lord Neville," Lady Southridge replied, nodding politely.

"My lord," Beatrix echoed.

"And what delightful diversions do you ladies have planned for the day?" he asked as he loaded his plate with much of the same as Beatrix, only a far more masculine portion.

"I'm not quite sure. I'm sure Bev and I will work on our embroidery," Lady Southridge answered.

Beatrix bit back a groan. Embroidery. How she hated it.

*Hated.*

"Perhaps we could take a walk, however?" Beatrix found herself asking, her tone pathetically hopeful.

Pride be cursed.

"Possibly, but I'd think that Lord Neville would need to make a trip to town today to check the post?" Lady Southridge shot him a meaningful glance.

"Indeed." He took a seat between Lady Southridge and Beatrix, though, she noted, his chair was noticeably closer to hers.

A grin tugged on her lips, and she lifted her teacup to take a sip, hiding her reaction.

"I'm not blind," Lady Southridge replied dryly, her gaze darting to the smaller space between her and Lord Neville.

"I doubt anyone has ever accused you of being such, my lady," Lord Neville replied, arching a dark brow and buttering a biscuit.

"Would you care for tea?" Beatrix asked him, sharing an amused glance.

"Please."

Beatrix poured his tea then paused, realizing she had no idea how he took it. How did a woman become betrothed to a man, ignorant of such a basic preference?

"No sugar, just cream if you please," he answered her unasked question.

"Of course." She added the milk and stirred.

"Thank you. To answer your question, yes. I do need to take a ride into town today. Would it be possible for you to spare your companion's company this afternoon so that she might go with me? With a proper chaperone of course," he added.

Beatrix bit on a crispy, salty strip of bacon and waited, praying Lady Southridge would agree.

"I see no fault in that. Do take a maid plus one other. While we are far into the country, word does travel, and we wouldn't want Bev's good name to be smudged."

"As you say, my lady," he graciously accepted then proceeded to eat his meal.

Beatrix was enjoying her eggs when a foot pressed against hers. Eyes darting to Lord Neville, she narrowed her gaze, but he gave no indication that he was aware of the close proximity.

Shrugging inwardly, she gave her attention to her tea, picking it up and bringing it to her lips. She gasped when that same foot slowly lifted the hem of her skirt beneath the table! Tea sloshed from her cup and stained the white linen tablecloth. As quickly as the hem of her skirt had been lifted, it was released, but the damage was done. Her gaze shot to Lord Neville, narrowing as she studied the way his full lips pressed together, as if restraining his amusement.

Miserable man!

Well, two could play that game!

With measured movements, Beatrix picked up her toast and took a bite, watching out of the corner of her eye.

"Do you think you'll receive word from London today, Lord Neville?" Lady Southridge asked.

He'd picked up his tea but paused to answer her question.

Beatrix set her toast down and slowly placed her hands on her lap.

"That is the very reason I have made plans to travel to town this afternoon," he affirmed with a nod. While he lifted his teacup to his lips, Beatrix made her move.

Before she could think better of her actions, she reached under the tablecloth and squeezed the underside of his thigh, as it was the only place she could touch him without being overly obvious, since the tablecloth only hid so much movement.

Her blush was immediate, but so was his reaction! Tea did not slosh; it practically flew from his cup, and if that weren't glorious enough, he choked on the liquid then sputtered and coughed into his quickly retrieved napkin.

Satisfied, Beatrix swallowed her laughter and forced her expression into one of sincere concern and turned to him. "Dear heavens, Lord Neville, are you well?"

"I — *cough* — am indeed — *cough cough* — Miss L — Bev." His dark eyes narrowed.

"Do be careful," she countered daringly.

"I will do my utmost, however..." He leaned forward slightly, matching her determination in his gaze. "...I find that sometimes one needs to take a risk or two."

Beatrix tilted her chin. "Indeed. For at times, the payoff is indeed worth it," she answered, glancing to his almost empty teacup and back.

"Touché," he whispered.

"In case you two had forgotten, I am still present." Lady Southridge's voice broke through their now silent engagement. "And I also feel it behooves you to understand I'm not as oblivious as you might imagine."

At this, Beatrix turned her curious gaze to the older woman.

Lady Southridge's light red eyebrows rose as if affirming her statement.

A fresh blush seared Beatrix's skin as she cleared her throat and straightened in her seat.

Then, with a barely restrained giggle, she turned to Lord Neville. "More tea?"

LORD NEVILLE COULDN'T STOP the smile that broke through at his memory of the escapade at the breakfast table that morning. Truly, Beatrix was a rare treasure. By all the saints, he still couldn't quite believe that she had squeezed his thigh! He was sure she'd had no idea the effect it had had on his person. She was far too innocent for that. However that didn't negate the fact that he'd needed to eat breakfast quite slowly, just to insure his own propriety.

Granted, he *had* initiated the whole thing.

But she had certainly ended it.

Further sealing her dominion in his heart.

The sound of the horse's hooves on the soft and moist

English soil were the only sounds of the moment. But it wasn't an awkward silence, rather a companionable pause between conversations that simply was like breathing, natural.

"If I weren't raised with the rain, I don't think I'd be able to tolerate it as well," Beatrix commented from atop her roan mare.

"Indeed." He had often thought the same. "Perhaps one day we'll venture somewhere slightly less… soggy." He glanced at the dark earth.

It was bloody annoying to keep their conversation so… bland. But with two footmen in tow, per Lady Southridge's directions upon realizing they were not taking the carriage, they had to keep up appearances.

A wicked smile twisted his lips. For surely it had to be wicked with the direction his thoughts took. "I find myself curious," he started as he turned to face Beatrix, her eyes narrowing as she studied his face, a slight edge of alarm peppering her expression.

He smothered a chuckle that threatened to rise.

"Yes?" she answered tentatively.

"What is your opinion of the floral gardens at Breckridge House?" he asked innocently.

A shadow of confusion crossed her expression before she answered. "I find them quite stunning."

"Indeed? I find that I share your opinion." He nodded, glancing from her to the road ahead. "But there is a particular species of flower I discovered in the orangery that has utterly captivated me. I find it's far more beautiful than any of the kind I've seen in London."

"Is that so?" Beatrix replied.

He glanced to her, watching as she studied him, as if trying to ascertain if he was talking about flowers.

"Its petals are so very soft, almost like velvet," he added, then, unable to resist the rake within, he offered her a quick wink.

Rising to the challenge as he'd known she would, Beatrix flushed and gave a disbelieving snort. "I would think you'd think the flower in question quite thorny," she shot back.

"At times. After all, even a rose has its thorns..." He shrugged. "...but I find that I don't mind a scratch or two. Sadly, however, I've been denied the pleasure of holding even one stem."

Beatrix choked slightly, as if scandalized at his comment.

"Are you well?" he asked as a footman glanced between them curiously.

"I, er... am." She shot daggers at him, only, rather than threatening him, it delighted him further.

"While the flower claims to be quite prickly, I'm sure that with the proper care, it will be utterly soft and supple." He hazarded a glance back to her, watching as her color burned deeper, though he'd believed that would be impossible just a moment before.

"I assure you that is incorrect. If we are speaking of the same species, that flower has a nasty bite."

"A flower that bites? Intriguing for certain. It's a good thing I'm not easily deterred, especially once I find something I need."

"Need?" she questioned, her tone softening only slightly.

He met her gaze, not blinking but responding. "Desperately."

"It's rare for a gentleman to admit that he needs something," she replied, a bit of a haughty tilt to her chin, as if questioning his motives.

"You'll find I'm not like most gentlemen." He bowed his head slightly.

"So I'm discovering." She flirted. "That and your affinity for flora and fauna," she shot back with a saucy grin.

"One type of flora." He grinned. "I'm hoping when we return to Breckridge House, Lady Southridge will allow me to study the specimen further." He allowed his gaze to rake over her luscious body, neatly packaged in an emerald-green riding habit that nipped and tucked at all the right curves. He turned to face the road, pleased at her gasp.

"I assure you that Lady Southridge is very… protective… of all things in her care."

"More's the pity." he replied. "I find myself dreaming of the velvet softness of the petals… the length of the stems and… the scent. It's quite heavenly. A delightful mix between rose and lilac with a hint of lemon."

When she didn't respond, he turned to observe her. A wide smile was threatening to break through as she shook her head, glancing heavenward as if petitioning for patience to deal with him.

"Do I try your patience with such a tedious subject?"

"I assure you, Lord Neville, nothing about you is tedious." Then she added in a whisper he almost missed, "Scandalous? Yes. Tedious? No."

The village came into view, with its straw-thatched roofs and stone buildings. Within the small town the Fox Inn served both as lodging and the post station.

"Do you wish to stop anywhere else, other than to collect the post?" He glanced over to Beatrix, riding remarkably well and once again tempting him with her delightfully attractive figure.

"No." She shrugged. "I have no need of anything else." Her brown eyes scanned the landscape before meeting his.

"Very well, I'll be back directly." He nodded and dismounted from his chestnut gelding, careful to tether the leather reins to the post beside the inn.

"Good day, my lord. How may I be of service?" a portly man with sparse grey hair asked, a hopeful gleam in his eye. His gaze quickly assessed Lord Neville, no doubt adding up his ability to add to his purse should he stay at the inn.

It was a different gentleman than the one who'd facilitated his prior stay, but they looked similar. Perhaps they were family?

Not that it was necessary, but he was always careful to catalogue such pieces of information. One never knew when they could become vital.

"Good day. Would you have any recent post that is addressed to Breckridge House?"

"Ah! Give me a moment. I'll see." The innkeeper nodded once and disappeared around a corner.

The familiar scent of bread baking mixed with the moist air hung in the inn. A moment later, the innkeeper returned, hands empty. "I'm afraid I have no post for the residents of Breckridge House. My sincerest apologies." And he did truly appear apologetic, as if afraid of offending the notable man in his small reception area.

"Thank you," Lord Neville replied, careful to hide his mixed emotion of confusion and concern. With a nod, he left the inn and strode out into the sunshine, but it was lost to his notice as his thoughts were preoccupied with possible reasons for Curtis's delayed response.

"Nothing?" Beatrix asked, pulling his attention from his inward contemplation.

He shook his head once and untied his mount. In one motion, he mounted his gelding and glanced to her. Turning way too quickly, he almost missed the tinge of pink that glowed from her cheeks. What had caused it?

"You're blushing." He led his horse close to hers, almost whispering the words.

"Am not," she denied, but as she turned to face him, it was all too clear that she indeed was.

"Liar."

"You—you— Why must you notice *everything*! Bah!" she huffed.

"It's in your best interest that I do," he reminded her gently.

Her gaze clouded slightly as she turned away, studying

the road. He hated that he'd caused that, but it had been necessary. It was a reminder for himself just as much as her; they needed to always maintain their diligent guard. Just in case.

But he didn't want her to carry the burden. Trying to distract her, he prodded her further. "Are you going to answer?" he asked then passed her as he took the road that led back to Breckridge House.

"Answer what?" she replied and encouraged her mount into a trot, coming up beside him.

"Why were you blushing?" he pressed, studying her face. Her skin even looked soft. As if remembering its texture, he felt his fingers twitch, wanting to touch her.

"I forgot." She glanced away.

"I believe we already discussed that you are not being honest when you say such things," he reminded, chuckling.

"And we already discussed your annoying behavior."

"But I didn't deny that accusation, if you remember."

She snorted softly then turned to him. "If you *must* know, I was… appreciating the view."

"Apprec—"

Her sudden urging of her mount into a lope as they headed down the road cut him off. It wasn't a full gallop, as it was difficult to maintain a seat when using a sidesaddle upon going at such a speed, but it was fast enough to leave him in the dust — rather, mud.

Urging his own mount to catch up, he had the advantage of a full gallop and caught up with her in a few moments.

"Don't run away. I'll just catch you," he spoke through a laugh as she narrowed her eyes.

"Don't I know it," she shot back then halted the horse quickly, and he blew past her.

"Damn the woman." He pulled up again, his horse sliding in the damp earth for a moment then stopping, chomping at the bit as if irritated at such a swift command.

He twisted in the saddle, its creaking leather punctuating his movement. She was riding at a sedate pace, flanked by the two footmen.

"Damn and blast." He shook his head. She was a crafty minx.

He turned his mount around and met up with the small party. "Enjoy your excursion?" he commented lightly.

"It was not nearly as productive as I would have liked," she replied with dry sarcasm, but her expression was one of amusement.

The sound of hoof beats stole his attention, and he glanced ahead of them, seeing a rider approaching quickly. "Stay behind the footmen," he commanded lowly to Beatrix and urged his mount ahead. Within a few moments, the livery colors from Breckridge House were plainly seen, and he relaxed his tightened posture. But why would Lady Southridge send out another footman?

"My lord." The footman bowed from atop his horse as he approached and stopped before him. At Lord Neville's nod, he continued, "Lady Southridge bids you hasten back to Breckridge House as you have a visitor who is most anxious to see you," he explained.

"Thank you. He turned his mount slightly to observe Beatrix's location. For a moment, he thought of returning quickly, leaving Beatrix in the care of the three footmen, but he didn't truly trust anyone but himself to her care. Whoever was visiting would have to be slightly more patient. "I'm afraid we'll have to increase our pace, if that is acceptable to the lady?" he asked, waiting for her nod.

They proceeded at a trot.

A bloody, pathetic trot.

Irritated, he encouraged his mount into a canter, hoping the party would take notice and increase their pace. Of course, they followed, but their canter was sadly lacking the speed of his mount.

His patience stretched thin, he pulled up on the reins, and, moments later, the footmen and Beatrix followed likewise. "If you'll excuse me." He smiled tightly and guided his horse around the flanking footmen and came alongside Beatrix's roan mare.

"Yes?" she asked, her expression full of curiosity as she tilted her head quizzically.

"Forgive me," Neville said as he quickly laid his leather reins aside. He reached out and quickly wrapped one arm around her waist.

Beatrix squealed but didn't fight his grasp.

Wise girl.

Immediately, he secured her with his other arm and situated her across his lap.

"Have you taken leave of every last one of your senses?" she spoke through clenched teeth as she struggled in his arms.

"Hmm, that actually turned out better than I'd planned." He shrugged and glanced to the opened-mouthed footmen. Clearly, they were at a loss as to the action they should take. After all, he was a peer of the realm.

A footman didn't exactly scold a lord.

"My lord…" one started.

But Lord Neville didn't give him a chance to finish his sentence. Nudging his mount's flanks, he urged his gelding to leap forward, carrying them toward Breckridge House at a much more satisfactory pace.

"You are mad," Beatrix ground out, even as she clung to him. "Have you any idea what you're doing to my reputation? Rather, what will be left of it from all the other situations you've created?" She elbowed him in the chest, punctuating her statement.

"I wouldn't do that if I were you," he replied, glancing to the swiftly disappearing ground beneath them.

"You are insufferable!"

"Why, thank you," he replied with a grin.

Brown eyes glared back at him, smoldering with a fierce anger that only added to his pleasure at the situation. She was nestled quite comfortably on his lap, his arms around her as he held the leather reins, directing his horse. The scent of rose and lilac surrounded him, a dangerous distraction as her arms tightened around his chest, as if questioning his grip on her.

"You'll not fall." He felt the need to assure her.

"Said the spider to the fly." She spoke with dry sarcasm. "If you weren't already so intent on marrying me, you'd be sealing your fate. I hope you know this."

"I'm aware. What's the worst that could happen? Lady Southridge demand I attain a special license and marry you directly?"

"I suppose, but you are also causing scandal. To think I once thought you reclusive and quiet," she muttered.

"Ha! I'm glad you've since then amended your opinion. I sound rather boring in that light," he spoke, chuckling at her scowl.

"Better boring than—"

"Bloody hell," he swore as Breckridge House came into view, the sight of a familiar carriage catching his eye.

"Pardon?" Beatrix smacked his chest, her tone scolding.

He glanced to her offended frown. "Pardon."

Her glower melted slightly as she studied his expression. "What is it?" she asked, her tone alarmed.

"It's Curtis," he replied, seeing no benefit from hiding the information from her.

"He traveled here rather than writing?" She rose up slightly to study the carriage as they approached the courtyard.

In doing so, she slid slightly against his lap, reminding him just how warm and soft she truly was.

No! He needed to rein in his own galloping imagination — heaven only knew how vivid it could be. There was a situation at hand that required all his focus.

But her bottom was proving to be very distracting, as well as the way she twisted, brushing his arm with her—

"No!"

"Pardon?" She shifted, damn it all, and faced him, one eyebrow raised in question.

"Nothing." He cleared his throat and tried to think of something, *anything* but her… and how she — *bloody hell.* He needed to distract himself lest he create far more of a scandal with his current state of impropriety! He needed to think of something he hated. Something like… "Turnips!"

"Did you just say turnips?" she asked, her brown eyes clearly debating whether he'd lost his mind completely this time.

"I… need to speak to the cook about turnips. Curtis hates them… loathes them really." Blast it all! Did he have to yell the damn word?

"That must be quite the aversion." Her eyes narrowed and studied him.

*In for a penny, in for a pound.* "It is." He nodded sagely and then pulled up on the reins, halting the horse just before Curtis's carriage.

Taking a deep breath, he contemplated cold turnips, mashed, no salt, sitting in a pot overnight till they— Satisfied with the effect of his musings, he felt at ease. Almost at once, he noticed the sound of their escorting footmen's arrival. A moment later, they were at Lord Neville's mount, assisting Beatrix from his lap. She slid against his thigh as they assisted her, bringing back all the desire from a moment before.

Heaven's above, he had to think of those blasted turnips again!

"Are you coming?" Beatrix asked when she turned and found him still astride his gelding.

"Yes." He nodded and dismounted. For once in his life, he was thankful for turnips.

# CHAPTER SEVEN

BEATRIX STUDIED LORD NEVILLE, TAKING IN his queer expression, a combination of disgust and desperation.

*Turnips?*

The man never ceased to be an enigma, and truly in this case, she didn't *want* to understand!

Cautiously, she studied the carriage in the Breckridge courtyard. The build was first-rate, clearly belonging to a man of means. No crest decorated the side, yet its absence actually drew one's eye to the craftsmanship of the carriage, its smooth lines and bold lacquered black.

"I see Curtis decided he needed another conveyance," Lord Neville spoke from behind her.

Turning she saw his study of the carriage, a rueful grin in place as he shook his head once.

Shrugging, she turned her attention to the stairs and ascended to the main entrance. Footmen stood by in their pressed livery, holding the doors open.

"I'm sure Lady Southridge has ushered him into a drawing room." Lord Neville's comment sounded more curious than certain, and Beatrix turned to glance at him.

"We could *ask,*" she replied dryly.

He cut her an annoyed glare. "Truly? Why, I'm quite humbled that I didn't think of that." His tone was wry.

"Another reason to be thankful for my presence." Winking at his irritated expression, she approached a maid and asked for Lady Southridge's whereabouts. Just as she was speaking, another maid approached.

"My lord…" She curtseyed to Lord Neville. "…my lady bids you join her in the blue parlor. You have a guest from London."

He nodded once and glanced to Beatrix, a winning gleam in his eye. He reached out an invitation to escort her, and she accepted, laying her gloved hand on his arm.

"You see, while I have found that while asking is a perfectly valid option, most often the information finds *you.*" His voice was more than slightly haughty.

Offering a sweet smile, she pinched his arm as her hand rested upon it.

But drat the man, he didn't even flinch.

"You'll have to try harder than that," he replied without even a glance in her direction.

Beatrix suddenly had the urge to trip him. Certainly *that* would be an example of trying harder!

But as luck would have it, the blue parlor came into sight, and her attention was absorbed with the sight of a gentleman pacing before the chaise lounge. Only a small profile of his face was visible, but it was already clear he was quite handsome.

"Damn it all, he's pacing." His voice was so quiet she assumed she wasn't supposed to overhear. A shiver of fear tickled her spine.

"Ah, my dear Bev and Lord Neville!" Lady Southridge caught a glimpse of their approach and stood, her expression one of relief.

"Neville." The gentleman nodded his head once sharply,

the universal masculine acknowledgement.

"Curtis…" Turning to Beatrix he glanced from her to the gentleman. "…allow me to introduce Bev—"

"Hang it all, Neville. Everyone already knows. Just call her Beatrix." Lady Southridge's irritated tone broke through his introduction.

His gaze cut to her then to Curtis. "Is that so?" His expression was dark as his brows drew together over his grey eyes.

"Indeed. Which is why I decided to visit rather than converse by post. We have quite the… dilemma. But if you'll please finish introductions." His amber eyes cut to Beatrix, expectant.

"Apologies. This is Miss Beatrix Lamont. Miss Lamont, may I introduce you to Mr. Curtis Sheppard."

"A pleasure." Beatrix forced a smile, but her heart had seized upon hearing the news that her cover was no longer in place. What exactly did that mean?

"The delight is all mine. As a gentleman, one can never tire of making the acquaintance of such a beautiful lady."

"*My* lady," Neville replied tersely, his tone more than a little possessive.

Beatrix held back a grin.

"Is that so?" Mr. Sheppard asked in a teasing tone. "Then that either complicates matters or solves them… depending on how you look at it." He rocked on his heels.

"Why don't we all have a seat? I've ordered a fresh pot of tea as well as refreshments. I do believe we will be taking residence in the parlor for some time." She ended with a resolute tone.

Curtis, Mr. Sheppard, took a seat in a wingback chair beside the fire, and Lord Neville led her to an opposing chair, one that was beside the chaise where he took a seat.

"Do share your news." Lord Neville leaned forward, resting his elbows on his knees.

Beatrix took a deep breath and turned her attention t‹ Sheppard.

"Miss Lamont, have you ever heard of a gentleman by the name of Sir Lambert Kirby?" He regarded her fully, and she got the impression that he was not a man who missed a single detail.

"No…" she answered.

"You?" Mr. Sheppard turned to Neville.

"No, I'm afraid not. Who is he?"

"That's the rub. According to him and to certain documentation presented at his local magistrate then brought to London, he is your cousin, Miss Beatrix. The son of your father's brother and, that being said, claims he has documentation that would include him in your father's estate through marriage to one of the daughters of the late Baron Lamont," he finished quietly.

"Pardon?" Beatrix felt her face scrunch in confusion.

"The bastard says he has the right to marry you to attain your fortune," Lord Neville spoke through clenched teeth.

Beatrix felt her eyes go wide as she studied Lord Neville.

"Well, that is absurd." She shrugged after taking a moment to settle herself. Smoothing her skirt, she turned to Mr. Sheppard. "My father did not speak with his brother. They were estranged. He died without an heir before my mother and father. And he certainly did not make a marriage contract between this… gentleman and myself."

"Miss Lamont, while I have not seen the documentation myself, that such a claim has passed from the local magistrate clear to London lends to the assumption that there is some validity to his statement. However, you are correct on one point. The marriage stipulation is not for simply you, but *one* of the Lamont heirs."

Beatrix swallowed, pressing back the urge to shiver at the thought of any truth to this man's claim. "But Bethanny is married, so that would leave myself and Berty, but she is far too young—"

"To be married immediately, yes..." He let the words linger.

Her heart stopped. "They could force her into a contract with a stranger? She's only ten!"

"Indeed, but contracts can be drawn up at birth, Miss Lamont."

"This is preposterous. And this is with the assumption that this — this Kirby gentleman is even valid in his assertion!" She stood and began pacing.

"Let us address a separate question for a moment. You said that there was no reason to continue her ruse because her whereabouts were already known. How did his happen? Especially when it took me quite a while to discover the truth myself," Lord Neville asked, his tone businesslike.

"It would seem that Sir Kirby has been scouring the countryside as well — rather, his men have been. It was only a matter of time, Neville."

"Damn," he swore quietly.

"So, if I'm understanding this correctly... Sir Kirby is out scouring the countryside for me, thinking he has the correct documentation to prove that I'm destined to be his wife, all so he can inherit my family's fortune. And if I refuse, then there's a chance that my little sister could be forced to enter into a betrothal contract with him?" Beatrix paused in her pacing, heart beating fast as her gaze flickered between Lord Neville and Mr. Sheppard.

"That about sums it up. Yes." Mr. Sheppard nodded once then stood. "But that doesn't mean that it is set in stone. He has no power to enforce anything at this point.

"Which works in our favor." Lord Neville stood as well, a determined gleam in his eye.

"Exactly." Mr. Sheppard tucked his hands behind his back and paced, his face thoughtful.

"What if... we give him what he wants?" Lord Neville

locked gazes with Mr. Sheppard, and both stopped pacing.

"You mean—"

"Yes."

"And then—"

"Quite possibly."

"We'll have to move quickly."

Lord Neville snorted. "Is there another way?"

"Not that I can imagine. Is she up to it?" Mr. Sheppard's gaze flicked to Beatrix then back to Lord Neville, searching for answer.

"Yes."

"Am I up to what? For heaven's sake, gentleman, will you please explain yourselves?"

"I do think that there's no other option." Lady Southridge stood as well, surprising Beatrix. She had quite forgotten the lady was present, so uncommon was it for her to be so silent.

"Am I the only one who has *not* gone mad?" Beatrix threw her hands down in a frustrated gesture.

"You, my dear, are going to London," Lady Southridge explained in a quiet tone, completely unnatural for her. Beatrix glanced to her beloved friend, a grandmother to her in so many ways.

"Why?"

"Because you have a wedding to plan." Lord Neville spoke darkly as he turned to face her.

"A wedding? You cannot mean for me to marry Sir Kirby—"

"Bloody hell, you are! You're marrying me. I do believe I've explained that enough the past few days. You truly are difficult on my ego, Miss Lamont." A small smile tipped the corner of his mouth, reminding her for a fleeing second of his flavor.

"I'm… confused," Beatrix replied, her gaze darting between the three people in the room.

"We're going to continue the ruse, only in a different

manner…"

"Oh heavens, no more *Bev!*" she all but cried.

"It wasn't that bad," Lady Southridge replied, her tone slightly offended.

Beatrix shot her a glare.

"No, no more *Bev.* You'll be Miss Lamont, but you're going to buy us some time with the ruse that you're open to the idea of marrying Sir Kirby."

"No."

"Yes."

"No." She stomped her foot.

"Did she just stomp?" Mr. Sheppard asked in an amused tone, but she paid him no mind. Her gaze was in battle with that of Lord Neville's.

"Yes. Because we need to solve this if you wish to ensure that you and your sister are completely free. This is the easiest and most viable solution. Curtis and I will address everything else, but we need time. Can you give us that, Beatrix?"

Her heart stilled at the sound of her name on his lips. His green eyes pulled her in, captivated her as he implored her, demanded, yet at the same time gave her the freedom of a choice.

"Yes," she whispered.

Lord Neville closed his eyes and nodded once. "Thank you." He met her gaze once more.

"There will be no shortage of sparks with you two, will there?" Mr. Sheppard replied, his tone a bit uncomfortable.

"You have no idea," Lady Southridge answered, her tone ironic.

"If you'll excuse me, gentlemen, I do believe I have to pack." She curtsied and turned to the door.

As she passed Lord Neville, he reached out and grasped her arm, pausing her exit. "We will get to the bottom of this, and you will *not* marry that man." He spoke with a determined edge.

She cut her gaze to meet his. "See that your promise is not idle. Because my sister will not be forced into such an arrangement. If you truly are set on my hand, you have no other option." She kept her voice resolute when tears threatened to make her weak.

Pulling her hand free, she quit the room and ascended the stairs, salty tears trailing down her face.

She'd allow herself one moment of weakness.

One hour of shedding tears.

Of feeling fear.

Then she'd put it behind her, face her future, and pray that Lord Neville would live up to the reputation he possessed.

He had to.

# CHAPTER EIGHT

"DO I DARE SPEAK, OR WILL YOU ATTACK?" Curtis asked with far too much amusement.

Cutting a scathing glare, Lord Neville rose from his frozen posture and strode meaningfully toward the low-burning fire in the grate. The scent of dry heat assaulted his senses as he stared at the glowing embers. The ladies had long ago retired after dinner, leaving him and Curtis alone.

"I didn't realize you had formed such an… attachment. I must say that after seeing you two together, however, I can see that you're quite firm in your convictions concerning your intentions. I simply wasn't aware that you were even more than acquaintances with the lady." Curtis's tone was conversational as he approached Neville's side.

"It started at the blasted Greenford Water's house party," Neville replied, taking a tight breath as he fought against the awareness of all that they would be risking in the near future with Beatrix at the heart of it all.

"Ah, was that the one where Graham—"

"Yes."

"Brilliant. Nothing like a house party to… hurry things

along."

Neville cut a glance to his friend, who raised a knowing eyebrow.

"Because you've been so close to marriage that a house party has enticed you to sacrifice your bachelor status on the altar of matrimony?" He knew his voice conveyed his tension. Damn it all.

"No, I cannot say I've had the pleasure of being so… enticed." Curtis's tone was light, but he turned away, shielding his expression.

Neville cocked his head in curiosity. Was there a lady who had somehow captured Curtis's attention?

Unlikely.

Which would make it all the more fantastic.

The whole idea that the bachelors most opposed to matrimony fell the hardest was indeed accurate.

And Curtis was one of the most dedicated bachelors he'd met in some time. Neville only hoped he was able to witness at least a portion of his fall. It would be undoubtedly epic.

"You do realize that your possessive behavior earlier cannot be repeated once we leave this estate?" Curtis replied, turning back to him, his face half-shadowed and half-illuminated by the fire's glow, adding a sinister twist to his words.

"I'm mindful."

"You cannot even be seen with her. It could jeopardize the entire operation." Curtis took a step toward him, as if trying to convey the importance of his statement.

"I'm bloody aware!" Neville all but shouted and, turning away, ran his fingers through his hair. "Hell… this is hell. Do we have anything on this Kirby bastard?"

"There's speculation, but—"

"Speculation doesn't produce results."

"Exactly."

"There's no other party that could have a motive to raise a

threat against the Lamont sisters. Sure he is behind—"

"That's the idea, the speculation… but without proof." He let the phrase linger.

"We could create a carriage accident…" Neville spoke in a low threat.

"And undermine your integrity? My integrity? No. And you wouldn't even if you had the opportunity."

Neville snorted.

"What's the damn plan? I'm assuming you have one." Neville pinched the bridge of his nose. Where was the brandy? He marched to the liquor cabinet, a rich mahogany side table, and withdrew a crystal bottle of the amber liquid he so desperately needed. Pouring himself a generous portion, he glanced to Curtis, raising his eyebrows in question.

"Please, and yes, I do have a plan. Thank you."

Neville poured another snifter and handed it over to Curtis.

Lifting his glass, he took a deep drink, letting the burn of alcohol ignite his throat and leave a fiery trail to his belly.

Curtis took a long sip and walked over to a chair. Sitting, he balanced the snifter on his knee, his fingers caressing the stem. "We'll leave in the morning with instructions for Lady Southridge to travel several hours after our departure. That way we are not associated. We'll take the road that circles around the back of London then approach it from the opposite direction than that of Lady Southridge, as if we were in an entirely different part of the country."

"Sounds easy enough, but what of when we arrive in London? We will have to work quickly to discredit Kirby's claim. You know that as soon as Beatrix is known to be in London, he'll be sniffing around her skirt. And with her directions to appear amicable to his suit…" His tone grew dark, and he knocked back the rest of his brandy.

"True, but women require wooing, do they not? He'll not expect her to agree to his suit immediately, especially with his claim still being validated before the regent."

"Heavens above, I hope so. Surely that would buy us some time. Do you know if he is currently a man of means, or is his only claim to fortune that which belongs to the Lamonts?" Neville asked then strode back to the brandy, where he poured himself another generous helping.

"Careful, old man. We need you to be thinking clearly," Curtis warned.

"When did you become my bloody keeper?" Neville shot back.

"Is Miss Lamont aware of your wicked temper? Or have you only shown your docile side, which I might add, I still question exists since I've never seen it with my own eyes?"

Neville growled.

"Brilliant." Curtis chuckled. "However, back to your question. From what I can understand from my sources, he is not a man of means, but neither is he destitute."

"Does he have a relation or friend in the *ton* who will insure his invitation to the various social gatherings that Beatrix will attend?" Neville swirled the brandy, inhaling its spicy scent.

"He has some connection to Lord Burgh, but it's questionable. They were seen in White's early last week, but when Kirby's hand won at cards, it was a considerable loss to Lord Burgh, and it is well known that he is not deep in the pockets presently."

"So that might cause a rift if there is any friendship. This is good."

"Indeed, but I left Henry with the express instructions to follow him upon my departure. I sincerely hope that he has additional information upon our arrival to London."

"Henry? Do you think he's up to the task?" Neville considered his friend.

"Yes. The lad has proven himself quite capable in the past few months. I felt it was a wise choice."

"Lad? The boy's nearly eighteen." Neville shook his head. "When did that become so young to us? Are we truly that old?"

"I'm not certain about myself, but you being of the ripe old age of thirty and one..." Curtis let the words hang in the air.

"Bastard. You're only a year younger," Neville replied with no heat, simply an irritated grimace. "But it's true that somehow... I'm ready. No, that's the not word... I'm..." He took a deep breath. "I was so reluctant to face the idea of marriage again after Mary and the situation surrounding it all... I simply wrote it off, thinking that marriage...that love was equal to those circumstances. But it's not. Maybe I am getting older, maybe I'm simply healing, but I find that Miss Lamont — Beatrix — has somehow shown me a completely different perspective. It's passion and heat, desire and lust, but it's also play, fighting, growing, actually enjoying the other person when she doesn't even like you... because even if she isn't to that point yet, you love her enough for the both of you... because you know she'll get there."

"That doesn't sound like you're a creeper." Curtis raised his glass in jest.

"Bloody hell, you know what I mean. She didn't chase me — hell, she didn't even want me. But it didn't matter because it only took a few moments, and I knew... I *knew.* How daft do I sound?" He gave a humorless laugh and shot back a large gulp of brandy.

"Like a lovesick swain."

"Brilliant. I always pitied those bastards."

"Well, if it makes you feel better, I pity you."

"Capital."

"But to be honest, when you two walked into the room earlier, the whole temperature shifted. One would have to be deaf, dumb, and blind not to see the spark — hell, the *fireworks* between you two! It was like Vauxhall Gardens! So often you see a man and his betrothed, and they are simply… boring! She stands with her hand on his arm, nodding and smiling, while he struts about, a pompous ass spouting his own miserable accomplishments, while the lady smiles sweetly and agrees with it all. Heaven save me from such a fate."

"Somehow I don't see Beatrix being that type of betrothed." Neville chuckled.

"No, which causes me no end of amusement. My wager is when this whole nightmare is over, and you are indeed the victor of the fair maiden's hand," Curtis stood and bowed in a theatrical fashion. "You two will create some sort of scene that will become the stuff of legends… some social faux pas that will forever shatter your reclusive lord status. I only hope I can have a front row seat." He lifted his glass as if toasting his own idea.

"That status served me well."

"Perhaps, but it's time for its end."

"I'm well aware."

"Then let us toast to the future and find our beds. Surely tomorrow will be upon us quickly, and we have much to do, old man."

"In truth, we do." Neville glanced to the final sip of amber liquid swirling in his glass. "And let us pray our victory comes swiftly."

"To a happy and quick ending." Curtis lifted his glass.

"To the end of Kirby's lies."

# CHAPTER NINE

"DO YOU THINK LORD KIRBY HAS approached the duke?" Beatrix asked while she swayed with the motion of the carriage as they made their way to London. Last night they had stayed at Hare Inn, and today they'd approach Town. It had been only yesterday that she had said goodbye to Lord Neville, yet it felt like far longer. Miserable man, he was even torturing her with his absence.

It was disconcerting, in the least, to even consider the reason for their trip to London. Was there any truth to this Sir Kirby's claims? Fear had led her to question what she remembered, what she had thought was so accurate. Was it possible she was wrong? Bethanny would surely know, as well as their family solicitor. Surely, the duke would take a protective stance.

Truly, she had no need to fear, yet, she did. Because various what-ifs circled in her mind, all stealing any security she could summon.

"I'm quite certain that the duke is fully aware of the situation. There's no need to fret, my dear." Lady Southridge reached over and placed a comforting hand over Beatrix's as it rested on her lap.

"Thank you. It's just that I — what if—?"

"What if is *not* what *is.* Remember that, dear. We can live another existence entirely if we simply dwell on what could be rather than what is. And if we do, it shall steal every ounce of joy from our lives, sucking us dry. Take each moment as it comes. Leave the unknown alone." Lady Southridge's gaze was shrewd and wise, adding to the direct tone of her voice.

"You are, of course, correct." Beatrix sighed then turned her gaze toward the window, watching as the countryside passed in a slow mix of green and grey.

"He'll not allow your fears to come to fruition. You know this." Lady Southridge's response pulled her attention back within the carriage. Turning to face her, she studied the lady's direct gaze.

"I know he'll try," Beatrix answered honestly.

Lady Southridge's expression grew amused as she shook her head slightly. "Then you, my dear, have never seen a man in love."

Beatrix withheld comment, choosing rather to ponder Lady Southridge's words.

The edge of London came into view, and they passed through the bustling city till Berkeley Square came into view. The hum of the city grew quieter as they approached the affluent area of residence within Mayfair. They stopped at the duke's residence on Grosvenor Square. Beatrix relaxed as she willed her body to quit swaying from the extended ride in the carriage. A footman liveried in the duke's colors opened the door and extended his hand for Lady Southridge's departure.

"Chin up, darling," Lady Southridge murmured as she exited the carriage.

Taking a deep breath, Beatrix followed and continued toward the entrance of the duke's London residence then ascended the various steps. Boxwoods lined the front, and the scent of rain and smoke hanging in the air reminded her that they were no longer in the country.

But in London.

Where everything had started, and now, hopefully, everything would end.

A familiar figure opened the door, causing her heart to do a little skip. "Murray!"

"Miss Beatrix? Is it truly you?" The old butler's face lit up from its usual stoic façade, and a wide smile caused his already-aged face to wrinkle further. Beatrix giggled and enveloped the old man in a hug, squeezing him tighter when he simply stood there. A moment later, she felt him return the embrace.

"You are truly a sight for sore eyes," he whispered hoarsely.

"Murray, you aren't crying?" Beatrix leaned back and studied the old man.

"No, no, of course not, Miss Beatrix." Shaking his head, he wiped away a tattling tear. "Your sister will be so very thrilled you are home. She's been a bit… out of sorts."

"Heavens above."

"And all the saints," Murray replied, a wink adding to his amused grin.

"Is she here? I swear if that's *not* Beatrix, I'll—" Berty's voice was interrupted.

"You'll do *nothing.* Am I understood?" Carlotta, Duchess of Clairmont, interrupted in her strictest tone.

She might be a duchess now, but she was originally Beatrix and her sister's governess, and, judging by the tone she used, Beatrix could only assume that she would never deviate from that role in their lives.

And Beatrix wouldn't have it any other way.

Carlotta had become their constant. She offered a comfort that helped heal the hole their parent's had left when they passed.

"Beatrix!" Berty ran down the stairs, a flurry of skirt and

ribbon. She leaped from the third stair from the bottom and slid along the marbled floor. "You're home!"

"Berty! How many times have I told you that ladies—"

"Don't jump, slide… or do anything of a diverting nature at all!" Berty called back with a more than disgruntled expression clouding her deep brown eyes, so alike to their older sister, Bethanny.

"Ladies do have fun," Carlotta called, grinning as she descended the stairs as well. Her delicate condition was far more pronounced than when Beatrix had left. "Beatrix!" Her expression was warm and welcoming, melting the icy fear that still tried to cinch around Beatrix's heart.

"Dry it up, Murray! No tears! Heavens above, and to think I once believed butlers didn't have emotions." Berty rolled her eyes but gave the butler a quick side hug before launching herself at Beatrix.

"I've missed you so much! Are you back to stay? Are you? Please say yes, and if you're not, I might simply kidnap you and tie you up, and I do believe that Murray will—"

"Yes, I'm back to stay, there will be no need to tie up anyone." Beatrix squeezed her sister, inhaling the familiar scent of lilac. "You've grown!"

"I have! Carlotta says I might even grow taller than you! Can you imagine? Me? The tallest of us all?" Berty released her sister, practically bouncing as she spoke.

"Yes, you might indeed." Beatrix grasped one of her youngest sister's braids and ran her fingers lovingly along the bumps.

"I do believe you're even lovelier than when you left." Carlotta reached out and pulled her into a gentle embrace.

The scent of rosewater clung to her skin, and Beatrix closed her eyes, remembering the comfort of Carlotta's genuine affection for her and her sisters. "You're too kind," Beatrix replied as Carlotta released her. "May I?" She glanced to her belly.

Carlotta nodded, a few blond curls bouncing with the motion. Her green eyes glowed with contentment and delight as she guided Beatrix's hands to settle over her precious bump.

"Astonishing," Beatrix whispered reverently as she held back a squeal of delight at the slight kick to her palm.

"Every day is a wonder," Carlotta replied, an awed lilt to her voice.

"Is he still in a panic?" Beatrix asked as she glanced behind Carlotta and down the hall toward the duke's study.

"Worse than ever." Carlotta rolled her eyes.

Beatrix withdrew her hands and glanced to Berty, who chimed in her opinion. "He's worse than a mother hen, or a grandmother goose, or a—"

"We get the picture, dear," Carlotta interrupted. Then to Beatrix she whispered, "How I regret her learning about metaphors."

"Where is Charles?" Lady Southridge bustled into the foyer, a determined sound to her stride as her genteel heels clipped along the marbled floor.

"Lady Southridge!" Berty exclaimed and promptly launched herself at the old woman.

"Ah, pet!" Lady Southridge squeezed Berty. "You're certainly taller than last I saw you!"

"Either that or your shrinking, Lady Southridge."

"Berty!" Carlotta scolded.

"It's true." Berty shrugged as she stepped back from the embrace.

"That's right. It is true, Berty. Though I'd be inclined to believe it's because you're taller." The older woman winked at Beatrix.

"I hope so. If you start shrinking, you'll be—"

"Berty," Carlotta clipped.

With a beleaguered sigh, Berty halted her thought mid-sentence.

"Impressive," Beatrix whispered to Carlotta. It wasn't common for Berty to actually not finish a thought.

"We've been working hard on that." Carlotta raised an eyebrow.

"Now, if I may ask again, *where* is Charles?"

Beatrix glanced to Carlotta. Charles was the Christian name of His Grace, the Duke of Clairmont. However, since Lady Southridge had contributed in large part to his upbringing, she had always simply called him Charles. The duke's parents passed when he was quite young so Lady Southridge felt compelled to step in. This only fostered the friendship between the young duke and Lady Southridge's much younger brother, Lord Graham.

However, as Beatrix had heard the story from both Lady Southridge's and the duke's perspectives, the duke would claim that the correct term was not *step in*, but *meddle*.

And based on the most recent history to which Beatrix could attest, *meddle* was probably the most accurate of the two descriptive words.

Carlotta's voice broke through her musings. "Yes, he is simply in his study. Murray?"

The butler snapped to attention at the call of his mistress.

"Would you please notify the duke that he has callers?"

"Indeed, my lady." With a crisp bow, Murray walked off, but not before he gave a quick wink to Beatrix.

"Now, the duke had mentioned a missive that arrived yesterday, but he'd not give us any other details other than you're immediate plans to arrive. What is exactly taking place?" Carlotta's pleased expression had melted into a concerned frown as she studied Beatrix.

"I do believe it will be easier if we discuss it with the duke so the situation doesn't require repetition," Lady Southridge answered, almost apologetically.

"I understand, I just… it's just that we had to send you off so quickly, and now you're back, thank heavens, but truly we are still concerned about your safety. That's the whole reason we created the ruse in the beginning… to protect you."

"I do believe our Beatrix has found quite the protector," Lady Southridge answered in her direct manner.

Beatrix gasped as her gaze shot to Lady Southridge, who appeared to be enjoying the moment.

"Protector?" Carlotta asked warily.

"Indeed." Lady Southridge raised an eyebrow as she met Beatrix's gaze.

"Finally! I say, how long have you ladies been out in the foyer standing about? You do realize we have parlors and such?" The Duke of Clairmont strode out, his dark hair and clear blue eyes a welcoming sight. As usual, his gaze settled on his wife before bouncing about to the other occupants of the foyer then quickly returning to Carlotta, who blushed under his regard.

"It's no wonder she's already expecting an heir." Lady Southridge shook her head, a wide smile stretching across her face.

"Lady Southridge! You cannot be so… direct. We have ladies we are trying to educate in the social graces… not the social underworld," the duke scolded.

"Never did I think I'd see the day he'd turn into such a turnip," Lady Southridge whispered to Beatrix. However, it was loud enough that everyone could easily overhear.

"I'm not a—"

"Dear?" Carlotta interrupted, no doubt saving them all from a futile debate. "Surely they are famished after their journey. Why don't we take a late tea in your study? Or the library perhaps?" Carlotta placed her hand on his arm, and he covered it immediately with his hand.

"Of course. Murray? Please send for tea and a late luncheon. And for any other callers, I'm *not* at home." He held Murray's gaze for a moment longer than was necessary, than was *usual*.

A shiver of foreboding tickled Beatrix's spine.

They made their way to the library, but, much to Berty's dismay, she was unable to join them. The duke had insisted she finish her studies, but Beatrix was rather certain it was because their forthcoming discussion wasn't for her ears.

As lovely as it was to age, there was something to be said for the ignorance of youth.

"Now, I assume you've heard the news of Sir Kirby and the case he is trying to present to the regent?" The duke dove into the heart of the matter as soon as the tea had arrived and the servants had been dismissed.

Carlotta was pouring tea and missed the cup slightly, telling of her own anxiety of the situation.

"We have been told about the allegations he has brought, stating he is the rightful heir of my family's fortune," Beatrix replied. "The difficult issue is that I don't remember him or the uncle that he mentioned. The question of his validity is a great one. Since upon my parents' death they couldn't find a next of kin, thus why we were given to you for guardianship."

"Indeed, I've considered the same. Do you remember any uncles, relatives of any sort? Perhaps he was born on the wrong side of the blanket? Which would not help his cause." The duke asked.

Beatrix shook her head. "Have you spoken with Bethanny?"

"Bethanny and Graham were here earlier and will be here tomorrow as well. She isn't familiar with Sir Kirby, which makes the fact that he's come this far with his allegations quite strange."

"So there's something we're missing." Lady Southridge nodded over her teacup, her eyes trained on the duke.

"I believe so. Lord Neville sent me a missive I received just yesterday," the duke started.

Beatrix heart hammered as the duke mentioned Lord Neville's name. For a few blessed moments, she had been able to push his memory to the back of her mind, but at the discussion of his name, all the emotion, the longing even the very scent of him was brought to the forefront of her mind.

"He was quite direct in his missive, possessive almost. Beatrix?" The duke speared her with his bright blue gaze.

She swallowed.

"Is there something we need to know?" he asked in a deceptively calm tone.

"Ha! Pardon. I shouldn't laugh, but if you two had been privy to all that I've been around the past week or so…" Lady Southridge shook her head, amusement thick in her expression.

"What do you mean?" the duke asked darkly.

"Don't get yourself into a lather. She's perfectly whole, if you gather my meaning."

"Heavens above, I'm so thankful Berty isn't here. I can just *imagine* what she'd start asking!" Carlotta remarked as she shook her head.

"I'm not in a lather, but it is my responsibility to protect—"

"The protector you spoke of… it's Neville?" Carlotta interrupted, her green eyes bright and excited.

"Protector? You certainly do not mean—"

"Would I let her become a man's mistress? Honestly, Charles, have a little faith in me!" Lady Southridge shook her head and sipped her tea in a haughty fashion.

"I know you too well to have faith in your schemes—"

"Oh, this wasn't in my plan. Well… I shouldn't say that. I rather wasn't certain if that part of my plan would work out, so it was more of a happy circumstance that worked out beautifully, don't you think?"

"How exactly, is it working out?" the duke ground out.

"Well, to be honest, he *had* taken quite extreme lengths to be assured of her hand—"

"What!" the duke roared.

"Sit down, Charles." Lady Southridge flicked a crumb off

her skirt. "As I was saying..." She shot a glare to the duke who was slowly sitting, all while glaring daggers at the woman across from him. "...he was quite brilliant, actually, but with the whole mess with Sir Kirby, his... intentions... are now compromised. But I foresee that becoming a boon for the whole conundrum." She nodded.

"So, if I'm understanding this correctly... Lord Neville, who has not approached me in any way—"

"To be fair, he's been out searching for Beatrix, with your blessing, I might add. Even though you knew the entire time where Beatrix was—"

"I'm bloo — blasted aware of where she was, but we needed it to look authentic! Just in case whoever was searching for her started to get wise to the idea. He was the perfect scapegoat."

"Indeed, he was."

"You made me forget my place, damn it all." He scratched his head.

"You were talking about Neville's lack of communication concerning his intentions," Carlotta informed him, her green eyes darting between Lady Southridge and her husband.

"Right, and so this gentleman, who thinks he has some right to be possessive of *my* ward, who hasn't spoken to me regarding his intentions—"

"You already mentioned that," Lady Southridge interrupted.

"So help me, if you interrupt once more, I shall gag you," he threatened.

"Empty threats. Charles, you've—"

"I'd not push him this time," Carlotta whispered.

"Ah, very well." Lady Southridge made a lock-and-key motion with her hand.

"If only," the duke mumbled, glancing heavenward.

"Ha!" Lady Southridge burst then covered her mouth delicately at the duke's glare.

"I missed this," Beatrix interjected, sighing.

"You're daft, but that's beside the point. And that point being, you are not spoken for. You are still under my authority, and I will not have you thinking yourself connected to this man in any way until the mentioned gentleman approaches me!" The duke nodded, seemingly quite satisfied with himself.

"Aren't you even the slightest bit concerned with Sir Kirby's intentions regarding myself? Here we are arguing about Lord Neville, and he's not the threat!" Beatrix shouted, standing and walking toward the low-burning fire.

"Sir Kirby is a windbag trying to make noise. He has no leg to stand on with his allegations," the duke huffed.

"Are we certain of that? Mr. Sheppard and Lord Neville seemed to be under the impression that he could possibly have some leverage or truth to his intention." Beatrix glanced behind her, watching the duke's reaction.

"We shall see, but I do know that you are in my care, under my guardianship, and to get to *you* Sir Kirby will have to go through *me*," he replied darkly.

"Well said!" Lady Southridge thrust her fist into the air.

"It is quite impossible for you to remain silent for any stretch of time, isn't it?" the duke asked, a surprisingly tolerant tone to his voice.

"It's part of my charm." She grinned. "However we must still tread carefully. As Neville had stated earlier, if he were to press his personal suit, it would only aggravate Sir Kirby, and we are not entirely certain he wasn't behind the original threat, so we must be ever vigilant."

"I'll not be expecting Lord Neville to be expressing his intentions anytime soon?" the duke asked.

"No, I expect not. Rather, I must amend that statement. I'm not quite sure *what* Lord Neville will do. He's been rather… surprising, I must say."

"Why do I get the feeling I will not approve of—"

"Because you're an old stick," Lady Southridge shot back.

"Can we please get back to the issue at hand?" Carlotta spoke in a commanding tone though amusement danced in her eyes.

"Here is the plan. I'll contact Lord Neville, request he inform me of his own findings regarding this blackguard, and we will determine how to move forward from there."

"Excellent," Lady Southridge approved.

"Agreed," Beatrix replied as well, feeling the need to at least say something since the whole sordid mess was about her.

"I do have one question," Beatrix pondered as silence descended on the usually loud group. "Has Sir Kirby approached you at all, Your Grace?"

The duke shared a glance with his wife. "It is of no consequence."

"Yes, I believe it is," Beatrix assured and turned to fully face the group. The heat from the fire warmed her back, keeping the chill of dread at bay.

The duke studied her for a moment then answered. "Yes, he has sought an audience with me."

"And?" Beatrix asked, letting her tone linger.

"And after I stated my opinion, he was told to never darken the door of my residence," the duke finished smoothly.

Too smoothly.

"He's continued to seek an audience with you, hasn't he?" Beatrix asked, though she was certain she knew the answer.

"Murray will not allow him entrance. You have no need to feel threatened."

Beatrix nodded, unsure as to how to continue.

"One thing is for certain. This Kirby fellow is not who he claims to be, this much we've already determined. However, you must never underestimate the desperate, and his actions speak of desperation. We must keep watch. And for that reason, Beatrix, you will not be allowed outside of the residence unless I am with you."

"I understand." Beatrix nodded.

"Now, I suggest we all take some time to freshen before dinner." The duke stood and extended his hand to his wife, gently lifting her hand to assist her.

"Come, Beatrix. I'll accompany you to your room." Carlotta smiled at Beatrix then glanced to her husband, squeezing his hand and withdrawing hers.

Silent, Beatrix followed Carlotta into the hall, her mind spinning in a few hundred directions.

The sooner they found the truth of it all, the better it would be. Hopefully, Neville had found something more substantial than she.

LORD NEVILLE RUBBED HIS eyes then focused again on the paperwork before him. Great stacks of documents littered his library, all of which pointed to the same conclusion.

Sir Kirby was exactly who he said he was.

Except for the fact that, deep in his gut, Lord Neville knew it wasn't possible.

How could a man suddenly appear with the perfect connection to the Lamont family when several years prior, such a connection didn't exist? It was common knowledge that the duke was only connected to the Lamont's through a hair's-breadth relation, but, surprising, all who had known him knew he took the guardianship of the three girls seriously. But if there was a closer relation, a closer connection, the duke wouldn't have been named guardian.

Sir Kirby would have.

Except he didn't exist.

At least not then.

Which meant that technically, he *still* didn't exist. Except that he did on paper.

Normally, the issue was to prove lineage through documentation, not the other way around. How did one prove that a gentleman didn't exist in direct contradiction to the documentation's proof?

"There's not enough brandy in the world for this," Curtis mumbled as he tossed a document on the ever-growing pile. "Bloody hell, this bastard is either a professional swindler, or he actually is authentic."

"I'm aware," Neville replied, studying the document before him.

"No wonder he's made it this far with such a wild claim."

"Indeed."

"You seem oddly calm… it's frankly far more terrifying." Curtis's voice was wary.

"Don't be such a nodcock. We simply have to be more intelligent than this charlatan. We…" Neville rubbed the back of his neck, taking a deep breath as he thought it through.

"Yes?" Curtis asked with an impatient lilt to his voice.

"…we need to draw him out… make him feel like he's won. So far…" Neville picked up another document. "…he's been meticulous, but no one is perfect. There's a flaw. We just have to find it."

"The proverbial needle in a haystack."

"Yes… what if…" Neville stood, stretching his aching legs. Slowly the dull pain dissipated as he paced about the room.

"Are you going to finish that thought, or must I wait in suspense forever?" Curtis drolled.

Neville shot him a dark look. "What if—?"

"You've said that."

"I would caution you against provoking me at this point. I find I'm exceedingly tempted to bloody someone up, pretending it's Kirby."

"Noted." Curtis nodded.

"We give him what he wants."

"Beatrix?"

"No—"

"But—"

"May I finish?" Neville paused and faced his friend, irritation bubbling within. Clenching his fists, he tried to remain calm enough to continue.

Curtis nodded.

"He doesn't want Beatrix. She is simply a means to an end. What he wants is her fortune. But in order to gain that fortune, he must first gain her. So we let him think he's won, or *will* win rather. Then, once he is settled in the idea, we destroy it, forcing his hand. You see..." Neville took a step forward. "...up till this point, he's been able to think through every move, every idea, every possibility." He took another step forward. "We need to destroy his rhythm, disrupt it. And, in doing so, he'll lead us directly to the truth of it all."

"You sound quite certain," Curtis ascertained, his expression skeptical. "It's quite the risk we take, that *Miss Lamont...* takes." He let her name linger.

Neville clenched his fists harder, willing himself to remain in control of his emotions when all he wanted to do was roar in rage and kidnap the lady.

But that wouldn't solve the issue. It would only create a new one that would forever mar their relationship. Unless the threat of Sir Kirby was abolished, Beatrix's freedom meant her sister's bondage.

And he couldn't allow that to happen.

Damn it all.

"Has Henry reported?" Neville asked, changing the subject.

Curtis raised his eyebrows in a telling expression but answered the question. "He'll be here sometime this evening, hopefully with some information we can use."

"He's been tailing Kirby?"

"Yes."

A knock on his study door drew his attention. "Yes?"

Stevens, his butler, entered with his usual ridged posture. "Mr. Henry is here to see you, my lord."

Neville shared a glance with Curtis. "Show him in."

"Of course."

Stevens left, and less than a minute later, Henry Sterling strode into the room. His light hair was cut shorter, giving him the impression of being older than his eighteen years. The boy had grown as well, Neville noticed, his height accentuated by his adolescent leanness. In truth, the poor kid looked like a string bean.

"Henry." Neville nodded.

"My lord… Mr. Sheppard." He nodded respectfully to the two gentlemen.

"We were just speaking of you. Do you have any information pertaining to this Kirby fellow?" Neville asked, studying the boy.

Henry's gaze was direct. "The man's a blackguard if I've ever seen one, but he's also keen. Kept on following him through Hyde Park. It was clear that he knew who to speak with, what to say, how to work the crowd as it were. His manners are impeccable, his tone genteel, everything you'd expect… when he needs to be."

"What do you mean by that?" Curtis asked.

"When he's with the betters, he acts as if he belongs. But he doesn't simply seek *their* company. I followed him into Cheapside then into a few more… compromising neighborhoods. He visited a bordello, a few gambling hells, and then made his way back to his lodgings, North of Oxford Street toward Paddington. Far more humble than that of Mayfair—if you gather my meaning—but respectable."

"All of this is not necessarily surprising, Henry. Is there any other information? Odd mannerisms? Tells when speaking to others, anything?" Neville asked, feeling desperation lick his heels.

The lad rocked back. "He's been to the duke's to inquire

about Beatrix."

"And?" Neville's jaw clenched as he imagined the slimy bastard even darkening the door of Beatrix's residence.

"And the duke sent him away shortly after he was granted an audience. But that's not the odd part." Henry leaned in slightly. "He keeps going back, every day, at the same time."

"Same time?" Curtis asked.

Henry nodded. "Same time every day, at the fashionable hour when the *ton* are out and about. With the duke's residence in such close proximity to Hyde Park, well, Sir Kirby gets an audience with every attempt… with every rejection," Henry finished, an eyebrow raised.

"But why would he want others to see his rejection?" Curtis spoke, his tone belying the question and making it more of a rhetorical statement.

"That is an excellent question." Neville threaded his fingers behind his head and paced toward the fire. "Why would a man want the very people he's trying to impress, to see his continual rejection?"

"He's sending a message. Perhaps it's not the *ton* he's concerned about, maybe it's the duke. Is he trying to convince him that he's not easily deterred, so much in fact that he doesn't care who sees his determination?" Curtis asked.

"If that were the case, then why would he make such an effort to converse at the park later, socialize, as it were?" Neville replied to the hanging question.

"It doesn't make sense."

"Nothing about this makes sense," Neville clipped.

Silence hung in the room, thick and deep like a fog. While Neville knew they were missing something important, he couldn't see it through the web of deception Kirby had expertly woven.

"We need time." Curtis broke the silence. Pinching the bridge of his nose, he sighed.

"I'll talk with Beatrix," Neville spoke.

"Like hell you will! There will be no contact! We don't want to force his hand too quickly, and if you are sniffing bout her skirts then—"

"I'll not be sniffing."

"You can't *not* sniff!

"If I might offer a solution?" Henry interjected, lifting a finger, but taking a step back when Neville glared at him.

"Any suggestion would be better than his idea," Curtis replied with an annoyed expression aimed at Neville.

Neville returned the glare, his own chest tight.

"Lord Neville, if you wish to write a letter giving detailed instructions, I can easily deliver it undetected and without raising suspicion," Henry offered.

"You forget that you've been tailing Kirby. Wouldn't he recognize you?" Curtis asked, giving voice to Neville's own thoughts.

"No, when I followed Kirby I took on the alias as a hack driver. It was easy enough to keep my distance once I recognized his routine. There are hundreds of hacks about town. I simply dressed like the lot of them, kept my head down, and made a few extra pence." Henry winked, a self-satisfied grin on his face.

"Wipe that arrogant expression off your face before I do it for you."

Henry didn't reply but sobered immediately.

"Do it." Curtis directed his words toward Neville.

Exhaling an irritated sigh, Neville glared at Curtis then stood and strode to his desk. Withdrawing a missive, he took a few moments to convey their message to Beatrix. Unable to help himself, even though he knew the risk was quite substantial, he used her familiar name, smiling slightly as he read, then re-read the word. *Beatrix*. To hell with the social sanctions that forbid her from receiving a letter from a gentleman. She *would* receive this one, and in it, see his determination, his vow that she would be his.

Not Kirby's.

*His.*

With a flourish, he signed his name then sealed the envelope with a glob of wax.

"Don't use your crest. We don't anticipate interception of the letter, but let us remain cautious," Curtis interjected.

Setting his crest down, he pressed his thumb into the warm red wax, leaving a print.

"Be off with you now," Neville commanded.

"Do I wait for a reply?" Henry asked as he tucked the message into his greatcoat.

"Yes," Neville replied, his tone daring as he glared at Curtis, who had begun to shake his head.

"Very good, my lords." Henry bowed and retreated, the sound of his footsteps down the hall the only reminder of his presence.

"The duke will not allow…"

"I bloody well know what the duke will or will not allow."

"…And the chances of her seeing the letter before him — hell, seeing the letter at all… Damn it all, we should have simply sent it to the duke. What were we thinking?" Curtis growled and stood.

"Regardless, they will gather the point."

"Indeed. You… you didn't add anything of a personal nature to the missive, did you?" Curtis paused and studied him carefully.

"I simply included that which we discussed." He shrugged.

"Very good." Curtis nodded.

"Now we wait, and I'm deuced sick of waiting," Neville spoke, irritation thick in his voice.

"That's what happens when you set a trap, my friend. You wait, pray, and watch. Believe me when I say we want to be alert for when we catch our prey."

"Let the games begin." Neville nodded, praying it

wouldn't take too long. Because each day, each hour, was one that separated him from Beatrix.

And that simply wouldn't do.

Not when the only place she belonged was in his arms.

# CHAPTER TEN

"MURRAY?" BEATRIX TILTED HER HEAD AS she studied the odd behavior of the butler as he shuffled his feet slightly and seemed to study something in his hands.

"Forgive me, Miss Lamont, but I—I have a missive for you, and I know that, well, a lady such as yourself shouldn't be receiving letters without the duke's knowledge, but... with you bein' so down lately, I thought that perhaps this is what you were waiting for?" He held out the cream-colored envelope.

It was true. Even with the earlier reunion with her eldest sister, her heart was heavy. Bethanny had mentioned the same in the short time they were able to be together.

Beatrix grasped the envelope from Murray's hand. There was no writing on the outside of the envelope. "How do you know its intended recipient is me?" Beatrix asked then flipped the envelope over and saw the wax, sealed with a fingerprint, no crest.

Could it be?

"There's a lad downstairs that is waiting for a reply. Now, I told him that there'd be nothing of the sort, ladies, such as yourself, do not—"

"Is he still there?" Beatrix asked as she quickly broke the wax seal.

"Er, I believe so, but I must advise against such an action—"

"Then go and find Carlotta. She will be my alibi — and yours as well." Beatrix winked at Murray, trying to allay his tension, but it was awkward for her, being so tense herself.

"Of course." Murray bowed and left to find his mistress.

Her eyes scanned the letter, taking in every flick of the pen, every word — especially one.

Her name.

Not her proper name, but her Christian name: Beatrix. Each letter of her name flowed carefully, as if the sender had taken great lengths upon the single word.

Her heart pinched as she ran her fingers over the paper, wishing that something more tangible than a missive connected her with Lord Neville.

But something was better than nothing.

So she'd be thankful for small blessings. Yet as she read the letter, her heart grew heavy with dread. She was to be welcoming to Sir Kirby. They had already discussed as much, but that she would be actually implementing such action made her stomach clench with dread.

But if this is what needed to happen in order to put to rest the entire situation, she'd do it gladly.

"Beatrix? What is going on?" Carlotta entered the room, her skin glowing with her increasing.

"It's instructions from Lord Neville, and, I'm assuming, Mr. Sheppard as well."

"And?" Carlotta asked, placing her hand over her swollen belly.

"And it's much of what we already anticipated. The only difference is that those words now need to become action." Beatrix handed over the missive, not missing when Carlotta's eyes widened as she surely read Beatrix's Christian name at the top.

Carlotta raised a skeptical brow but continued reading.

"We are to allow Sir Kirby to pay you court?" Carlotta spoke with a sharp tone of derision.

"It would seem so, but I have all confidence that such action will not be in vain," she asserted.

"The duke will not be pleased." Carlotta bit her lower lip as she seemed to re-read the letter.

"The duke will know that such an endeavor will be to the benefit of us all and give Lord Neville and Mr. Sheppard the time and circumstances needed to sort this whole thing out," Beatrix emphasized.

"You have great confidence in Lord Neville." Carlotta lowered the letter and regarded her with a clear green gaze.

"I do."

Carlotta studied her for a moment longer. "Do we need to reply?"

"Murray said there was a lad waiting."

"Give me a moment." Carlotta turned to walk away.

"Wait!" Beatrix followed after her. "Please, allow me to write it. You can stand behind me. Only let it be in *my* hand."

Carlotta turned and considered her. "Why? And do not think for one moment that I missed that the letter clearly stated your given name, my dear. Such a liberty isn't to be given freely. I know you must understand." Carlotta narrowed her eyes.

Beatrix squared her shoulders, not willing to cower under her practiced governess's eye. "I'm aware… but this, this letter is the only connection I have at the moment. Please, I beg you. Do not deny me this small indulgence."

Carlotta glanced from the letter to Beatrix then back. With a sigh, she extended the letter. "Then be about it quickly."

AS PREDICTED, THE DUKE was not pleased with the letter's contents, least of all the request that Beatrix be allowed to be in the presence of Lord Kirby. But after his temper had cooled slightly, he understood the implications of its benefit in the long run. "Just because I understand does not mean I have to like it," the duke huffed indignantly as he paced about his study. "If I had my way, I'd not let the gentleman near you." He glanced at Beatrix.

"Surely Lord Neville and Mr. Sheppard have a reason for such a request, my lord. We must trust them."

"Trust, ha! I'll trust Neville when he asks *my* permission to address you by your Christian name!"

"I highly doubt you have much to fear since the gentleman in question cannot even be near me while this Kirby farce continues," Beatrix replied, her tone terse as her patience ran thin.

She studied the Aubusson rug with its beautiful design of blue and red, trying to focus on anything but the irritation grating on her last nerve.

"Your grace?" Murray entered the study and, as if sensing the tension in the air, took a step back.

"What is it?" the duke snapped.

"Your grace, you asked to be notified when Sir Kirby arrived? The gentleman in question is requesting your audience." Murray bowed slightly.

"Please let him know that if he wishes to have an… *audience…*" He stressed the word. "…he'll have to take it tonight at the Smother's rout." As soon as the duke finished the word, he shot a glare to Beatrix. "Like *hell* will I let that snake around you without the whole of the *ton* as witnesses. It will also act as a precautionary net. He'll be needing to follow every social protocol, which should render you quite safe." His tone gentled as he gave a final nod to Murray, who left to report the message.

"I see. That was very… discerning, Your Grace," Beatrix

replied, humbled that he had put so much thought into the situation.

"You're in my care, under my protection. I—I care Beatrix. So help me I will do all in my power to keep you safe." The duke closed his eyes then sighed. "You have my leave. But please be ready to attend Smother's Ball tonight. We have work to do." He shot her a direct gaze that left her chilled.

"Yes, Your Grace." Beatrix stood and with a curtsey, left.

As she passed down the hall and toward her room, all she could think was…

*Let the games begin.*

# CHAPTER ELEVEN

"YOU ARE COMPLETELY CERTAIN THAT THEY will all be in attendance tonight?" Neville asked again of Henry.

"My lord, I have heard it directly from Kirby's lips. If I were to get any closer to the source, I'd have to have been touching the gent, and, my lord, I'm not that type," Henry joked.

Neville glared.

Henry cleared his throat. "Yes, I'm certain."

"Thank you. That will be all." Neville dismissed the lad, his gaze focusing on the fire, seeing the glow but not focusing on the flames. Like the heat from the blaze, his blood burned just knowing that Kirby would have the opportunity to make Beatrix's acquaintance.

Jealousy burned like a savage beast.

Temptation presented itself in the most basic way, but did he dare risk the operation?

Surely the duke would protect her, would he not?

But was that a risk he was willing to take?

No.

From that point on, it was easy to convince himself that his presence at Smother's Ball was absolutely necessary. No one had to know he was there.

Except her.

Most certainly, Beatrix would know. He'd make sure of it.

Their courtship was anything but normal, but that didn't make it less authentic. But he was certain of one truth; she needed to see his devotion to her safety, her protection. What sort of husband or lover would he be should he not offer the safety of not only his name, but his body?

She needed to know, in the most elementary way, that he was there for her.

Rather, *he* needed her to recognize it. To prove it.

Settled, Neville strode from the room, the fire crackling and accentuating his determined stride as he ascended the stairs.

"Strout!" he called, shrugging out of his coat and tugging at his cravat as he pushed open the heavy wooden door of his chamber.

His valet's silver head ducked out of his closet, an expectant expression coloring his aged face.

"My evening kit, if you please," Neville clipped. With any luck, Smother's Ball would be a crush, and no one would even notice his arrival. A grin spread his lips as a different plan took form in his mind. "Wait. I've got another idea."

BEATRIX BREATHED IN DELIBERATELY, trying to calm the racing cadence of her heart. Truly, she wished to be anywhere but where she was, but no other choice was offered. If she didn't walk this road, it would risk her sister's freedom. Glancing to the floor, she caught a glimpse of her fingers, tapping her thumb nervously. Immediately her thoughts centered on Lord Neville. How she wished he would be in attendance as well. Yet she knew it was impossible.

The ballroom glittered with flickering candlelight; yards of silk accented the rows and rows of hothouse roses. Smother had put forth an exemplary effort to employ every sense of the arriving guests, from luminescent décor to the heady scent from the floral arrangements; it was delightful and a welcome distraction from the impending introduction.

"Be brave," Lady Southridge murmured from her right. With Carlotta in confinement due to her delicate condition, Lady Southridge was her chaperone along with the duke. Bethanny and Lord Graham would also be in attendance, lending her further allies. It was all so strange. Beatrix continued to study her surroundings, taking in the elaborate gowns of the ladies and the perfect black lines of the gentlemen's evening wear. It was odd without her own debut behind her, but there was no way to rectify it. Already London was abuzz with the news of her arrival, especially with her earlier departure such a mystery cloaked in rumor and suspicion.

Hushed whispers followed her as she made her way through the wide ballroom with its highly polished marble floors. Thankfully, Carlotta had staved off much of the speculation with the story of her accompanying Lady Southridge to her country estate, but it was inevitable that others would doubt its validity.

Especially with Sir Kirby making no intention to hide his efforts to secure her attention through the duke. Could her life become any more complicated? All these sensations and emotions wove a fog-like spell about her, but none of it dulled the pain of loneliness that one experienced when missing the one who had stolen her heart.

Stolen was an accurate verb. She breathed a gentle laugh as she remembered Lord Neville's anything-but-subtle pursuit of her. What she wouldn't give to simply know he was near.

"Are you well?" Lady Southridge asked, pulling Beatrix's thoughts back to the world around her.

"As well as can be expected," Beatrix replied with a dry tone.

"Brilliant, seeming as you're about to meet Lord Kirby." Lady Southridge breathed the words so silently she almost missed it.

"Exc—"

"Ah, Sir Kirby." The duke's voice interrupted her. His tone was far from polite.

"Your Grace."

Beatrix fixed her gaze upon the man before her. Impeccably dressed, Sir Kirby held a ridged posture, as if bracing for a verbal sparring. His eyes, a muted-brown, didn't stray once to Beatrix but fixed on the duke as if evaluating an opponent. He was of a similar height to the duke, but far less substantial in presence, causing him to appear much smaller. With a pointed nose and angular cheeks, he wasn't a handsome man, but neither was he offensive in appearance. Rather, Sir Kirby was simply… average.

Beatrix studied him, curious as to his reaction to the duke, yet trying to catalogue any detail that may be of use in defeating this unfamiliar enemy.

"May I offer the introduction of my ward, Miss Lamont?" The duke's tone was frosty like a January morning, dry and without any warmth.

Finally, Sir Kirby's gaze flickered to Beatrix then back to the duke.

"Indeed." He raised a thin eyebrow. "I'll wish to secure a waltz with so lovely of a lady."

She glanced between the duke and Sir Kirby, curious as to how he could have developed any opinion on her loveliness when he had scarcely spared her a glance.

Not that she minded.

But she did *wonder.*

"A waltz would not be permissible. You see, my young ward has not officially had a come out, and with the ladies of

Almack not having given their permission…" He let the words linger in their implication.

"Of course, we would not wish to offend propriety." Sir Kirby remarked, rocking slightly on his heels. "A reel then."

"A reel, it is." The duke nodded once then extended his arm to Beatrix, all the while staring down Sir Kirby.

Taking his arm quickly, the duke escorted them away from the strange man and into the crowd.

"The man gets under my skin. There's something off about him," the duke remarked, primarily to himself.

"He didn't even look at me," Beatrix replied.

"He gazed at you plenty when we first arrived," the duke growled.

"Oh." Beatrix felt shiver of icy dread slowly trickle down her spine.

"So help me, if that…" The duke seemed to catch himself before speaking out of place. "He better not try anything during the reel."

"I would imagine it would be quite difficult to try anything untoward during such a lively dance," Lady Southridge interjected.

"Snakes are cunning," the duke answered.

Lady Southridge agreed. "Indeed."

The music began, and Beatrix watched in stunned silence as the dancers lined up in the open space on the ballroom floor. The cotillion began, a swirl of color and movement that momentarily stole her worry.

"There you are!" A wonderfully familiar voice called to her, blanketing her in a calming peace.

Turning, Beatrix barely restrained herself from running into her elder sister's arms. Ever dashing, Lord Graham stood protectively near her sister, a golden angel fiercely devoted to his wife.

"Bethanny!" Beatrix cried, not caring that she drew the attention of those nearby.

"You are so beautiful." Bethanny was careful to embrace her sister without crushing their gowns, all while murmuring the endearment.

"As are you," Beatrix countered.

"I take it you restrained yourself and didn't throw fisticuffs?" Lord Graham's tone was wry but amused as he directed the question to his friend, the duke.

"No, I was civilized," the duke replied.

"Barely," Lady Southridge added.

The duke gave her a dark look.

"I didn't say I disapproved. I rather would have enjoyed seeing you bloody up the bastard."

"Lady Southridge!" Bethanny scolded.

"It's true." The dowager hitched a shoulder, obviously uncaring of her breach of social protocol.

"Here, here!" the duke encouraged.

"The lot of you are mad." Beatrix glanced heavenward, then turned to her sister. "I'm to dance a reel with him."

"A reel? That isn't as threatening as waltz," Bethanny asserted.

"She hasn't had a proper come out, so we have protocol on our side," Lady Southridge explained.

"Brilliant," Graham spoke approvingly.

The music for the cotillion ended, transitioning into a Scottish reel. Heart hammering, Beatrix glanced from the duke to Bethanny, seeking strength.

"You can do this." Bethanny reached out and held her sister's shoulder with her gloved hand.

"I know." Beatrix inhaled deeply through her nose and turned slightly, watching the approach of Sir Kirby.

"My lady?" He held out a white-gloved hand, a look of expectancy in his eyes.

"Sir." Beatrix grasped his hand and followed him onto the dance floor. Her back burned with the gaze of the *ton* as conversations halted when they passed. The music picked up, and she found her place in the reel. Through the entire set, she felt an air of expectancy for Sir Kirby to speak to her, even speak one word during a turn, but he did no such thing. Rather, his inscrutable gaze watched her, detached and almost bored.

It was anything but the regard of a man in pursuit of a woman. As the reel continued, her gaze strayed to the crowd. The faces blended together in a rainbow of color, but as she walked down the line, her skin prickled with awareness. She glanced to Sir Kirby, curious if his level of attention had shifted, but his gaze was directly before them, stoic and stern.

Casting her attention to the crowd, she scanned for a particular gaze, simply out of sheer desperation for its presence.

Then, a glimpse of the familiar shocked her! Grey eyes met hers then blended into the crowd. Blinking, she tried to find them once more, but failed.

Heart beating with hope, she misstepped at a turn, earning a confused glance from her inattentive partner, Sir Kirby, but nothing more. As the music ended, she curtseyed and fully expected Sir Kirby to escort her to the duke.

"Take a turn about the room with me," he asserted, giving her no other option as he placed his hand over hers and led her to the edge of the ballroom.

"I do not think you have gained my guardian's permission—"

"I do not need your guardian's permission, Miss Lamont. I'm within every social constraint to take my dance partner about the room en route to her guardian." He added the last line, surely trying to cloak his earlier demand.

"Sir Kirby, I find your attention confusing." Beatrix spoke plainly, pausing mid-stride and facing him.

He halted and turned to her, his expression clearly shocked and frustrated. "I care not for how you interpret my actions," he spoke, equally as plain.

"If you have no regard for me or my opinion, then I would have to deduce that you have no intentions of pursuing the matter of my acquaintance further," Beatrix tried, knowing it was a long shot.

He gave a condescending chuckle. "Ah, the endless amusement of the female mind." None too gently, he tugged her along till she had no choice but to walk beside him.

"I take umbrage to your remark, sir."

"And I care not."

"What *do* you care about then?" Beatrix halted gain, pulling her arm free and facing him.

"Obedience…*Revenge.*" He bit out and squeezed her wrist painfully as he made no qualms about his belief on the matter.

"Then you shall find me disagreeable indeed," Beatrix bit out, trying to ignore the pain.

"Perhaps your sister would be more amicable," he offered in a veiled threat.

"For one to claim to be close enough of kin to have rightful ownership of our wealth, you certainly do not know the nature of my family."

At this, he simply smiled, a wicked, cold amusement that chilled her blood.

"If you—" Beatrix started but was unable to finish as a footman plowed into Sir Kirby, his tray laden with lemonade!

The two men tumbled onto the ground, a loud crash of shattering glass accenting their fall. Lemonade pooled beneath them, offering up its sweet and tangy scent.

"You imbecile!" Sir Kirby shouted, sitting up and brushing off his evening kit with an obsessive desperation.

"A thousand apologies, my lord," the footman offered, but the voice was oddly familiar, as if…

Familiar grey eyes darted up and met hers, flickering a connection of awareness, conveying a secret message meant entirely for her.

Unable to stifle the grin that broke out across her face,

Beatrix bit her lip and turned away, knowing she needed to gain control of herself lest Neville be discovered.

Though, upon quick reflection, few would expect an earl to dress as a footman.

Just another reason she was captivated by the enigma of Lord Neville.

"Bastard," Kirby swore as he glared daggers at the footman-liveried Neville, who had taken on an extremely contrite pose as he struggled to assist Sir Kirby.

"A thousand apologies, my lord!" Neville replied, his voice a mix of nasal and cockney.

Kirby brushed off Neville's attempt at aid and stood then took a step away from the disaster. Even though they were at the edge of the ballroom, the ruckus was enough that people had begun to gather.

Beatrix studied the small circle of lords and ladies as they murmured behind hands and fans, studying the mess, condemning it. Her heart pinched. Would they recognize Lord Neville in his disguise?

"I'll see to it that you're dismissed immediately," Sir Kirby threatened, brushing off his sleeve with a white linen handkerchief. With a withering glare, he stormed away, likely to depart since he was soaked through from the incident. Surely his threat was in earnest; however, little did the man know that the footman was anything but employed by the Smothers.

Neville glanced to Beatrix then behind her and back once more. Narrowing her eyes, Beatrix turned and followed where his gaze had landed. Upon seeing a balcony in the far corner, she turned back and gave the smallest nod of understanding. Neville stacked several broken shards of glass upon his silver server and walked away, the crowd giving him a wide berth. Several other footmen arrived at that moment with a maid in tow to address the rest of the mess. No longer interested, the multitude dispersed, leaving Beatrix ignored once more.

Not wasting a moment, she lifted her cream-colored gown just above her slippered feet and stepped over a few remaining shards of glass and started toward the balcony. Heart hammering with delicious expectation, she glanced behind her to ensure she was not drawing attention then continued on her way.

The hall grew darker from the absence of the multitude of candles, and as she passed the final pillar leading to the balcony, a hand reached out and pulled her behind the ivory support.

A scream on her lips was stilled as the intoxicating tone of Lord Neville's voice crooned in her ear. "At last. Where you belong."

Relaxing into his embrace, she took a breath, soaking in the moment, stolen as it was.

"I've quite decided that I'm going to kidnap you and your sister, putting an end to this whole charade." Neville chuckled, wrapping another arm around her waist, cradling her against his warm chest. The scent of lemon hung in the air, adding humor to the otherwise emotional moment.

"Is that so?" Beatrix asked.

"No, but I'm running out of patience," Neville answered darkly.

"As am I. And I must take a moment to assure you that should lurking in dark shadows at night and masquerading as a gentleman by day should fail you, the option of becoming a footman is not a venue you should entertain," she teased.

He tsked his tongue, a smoldering heat to his direct gaze. "And I thought my skill was unparalleled in that arena."

"Thank you, by the way," Beatrix replied, humor vanishing as she remembered the painful grip of Sir Kirby.

"The bastard is lucky to be alive right now," Neville responded menacingly. "It was clear to see the pain he was intentionally inflicting on your person." Releasing her, he coaxed her to turn and, in the soft light, lifted her wrist and studied it for injury. Tenderly, he raised the still sore flesh to his lips and kissed it ever so lovingly.

"Much better," Beatrix whispered, her heart thumping wildly at the care and regard he lavished on so small an injury.

Lifting his gaze, he studied her face. "Come." He held out his hand.

Taking it, she followed as he searched the hall then pulled her along it a few steps and into a shadowed corner concealed by an impressive tapestry.

"As much as I wish to discuss anything but Sir Kirby, I must ask, have you learned anything new?" Neville asked as his hands drew lazy circles upon her wrist.

Taking a shaky breath, Beatrix pulled her senses into focus. "No, have you?"

His gaze darkened. "Not enough. But we will find something. We just need time, but after seeing his handling of you, I don't wish to continue as we intended."

"He holds no regard for me, for my family. It was odd." Beatrix shook her head slightly as she considered Sir Kirby's reactions and actions before and during their dance.

"What was odd?" Neville's gaze sharpened.

"He — Sir Kirby —hardly spared me a glance. For one so determined to attain my family's fortune through marriage, I would have expected a bit more… interest?"

"That is odd. You're a rare beauty. I know that I could scarcely keep my eyes off of you." Neville pulled a hand up to his lips and kissed it.

"Charmer." Beatrix raised a daring eyebrow. "What was stranger was his attention to the duke. It was odd how he paid such close attention to him, like he was the person of interest."

Neville blinked then glanced down at the floor as if considering a difficult equation.

"I had not considering that aspect," he spoke softly. "It… has merit. I cannot think why I hadn't thought to connect the two." He released one of her hands and rubbed the back of his neck.

"Do you think there's a connection between the duke and Kirby?" Beatrix asked.

"I don't know… but I never thought to look. I need to take my leave." Neville released her hands and took a step away then paused. Turning back to her, he reached out and, in a flash, she was back in his arms, his grip both demanding and gentle at once as his lips found hers, invading, pursuing her in the give and take of love's kiss.

Melting into the moment, Beatrix gripped his shoulders, pulling him in tighter, closer, not caring that he was surely crushing her dress. His kiss grew more demanding as he invaded her mouth, branding her with his unique and addictive flavor. Her hands roamed his back, tracing his shoulders through the livery he still wore and moving up to grip the soft seductive texture of his dark hair as it threaded through her fingers. He groaned as she tugged on the strands, leaving her lips and trailing hot kisses down her jaw to her neck, rendering her breathless.

His breath hot at her collarbone, he paused, resting his head against the curve of her neck. Gasping, Beatrix closed her eyes, memorizing the sensation of his body so close, the scent of cinnamon and lemon etching itself on her memory.

"This is far too significant, too rare to allow time to be sifted away from us." He lifted his head to meet her gaze. His expression was open, as if trying to share his very soul. Gently his fingers ran down her face, leaving a warm trail on her sensitive skin. Pausing at her lip, he traced their shape. "Mine," He murmured a moment before kissing them once, lingering.

"Mine," Beatrix whispered unwilling to let this stolen moment pass them by, she captured his lips. At once he took command of the kiss. The world around faded, leaving on him, his flavor and the heat from his body as he pressed into her. Yet she tasted a restraint and gently he ended their passionate exchange. Not ready for their moment to end, she lifted her hand, she tugged at his hair seductively then trailed her hand down his jawline to his lips where she whispered once more, "Mine." Sealing the words with a final kiss, she lingered.

"Beatrix?" Bethanny's voice called out quietly.

Neville kissed her once more then took a step back. Meeting her gaze with a smoldering one of his own, he stepped out into the hall. "She is here."

"Pard — oh." Bethanny's voice was stilted, as if unsure with how to continue.

Chuckling slightly, Beatrix followed Neville into the dim light of the hall, further amused by her sister's shocked expression as it darted between herself and Neville.

"I—I—"

"Do not be distressed, Lady Graham. Your sister was not consorting with one of Smother's footmen." Neville chuckled darkly as he approached Bethanny, Beatrix at his arm.

"Neville?" Bethanny breathed.

"The one and only," he answered quickly with a bit of an arrogant air.

Beatrix attempted to elbow him in the rib, but he sidestepped perfectly. "I know you well, love." He turned to wink, even as Bethanny gasped in surprise.

"Too well apparently." Beatrix narrowed her eyes slightly, but was unable to restrain her grin.

"This is unexpected." Bethanny found her voice and folded her hands before her.

"Is it truly?" Neville asked, shaking his head then tossing a quick grin at Beatrix.

"I must say you cut a dashing figure as a footman," Bethanny retorted.

"I've been told."

Beatrix elbowed him again, this time hitting him square in the ribs.

"Foul." He glared at her.

Giving him a saucy wink, she simply turned her attention to her sister's confused yet amused gaze.

"I'll leave you to your sister's care until later." Neville reached out and held onto her hand carefully, placing a kiss to her wrist every so tenderly. Then he disappeared into the shadows.

"I don't know whether to be shocked, angry, scandalized, or simply… amazed." Bethanny blinked as Beatrix started toward the ballroom.

"He has that effect on people," Beatrix replied with dry humor.

"You were quite… familiar with him." Bethanny cleared her throat as if uncomfortable approaching that particular topic with her younger sister.

"One is normally familiar with the gentleman they intend to marry."

Bethanny's silence echoed for a moment. "That is true. Is the duke aware of this intention?"

"Yes, however, Neville hasn't exactly asked permission," Beatrix replied.

"Which, I would imagine, has caused the duke's distain toward him."

"But to be fair, he didn't actually ask me either the first time… rather, told me." Beatrix shook her head.

"Pardon?" Bethanny stopped mid-step and turned to her sister.

"Neville tends to… determine a course of action and assume there will be no opposition to that particular course… and if so, that opposition is unimportant. Needless to say, it has given me no small entertainment to completely upend his world." Beatrix chuckled.

Bethanny joined in. "I would imagine that would be quite diverting."

"Certainly, it is… and I would imagine it is why his

attachment to me is so firm," Beatrix remarked.

"It would undeniably appear his attachment to you is quite… determined." She turned to her sister. "Was that *Neville* who created the ruckus in the ballroom?" Eyes wide, Bethanny pieced the puzzle together before Beatrix had the opportunity to nod.

"It was. He saved me from Sir Kirby's overly possessive grip of my person. That man is wicked." Beatrix rubbed her arms, chafing them against the sudden chill of Sir Kirby's memory.

"He was your guardian angel," Bethanny replied, a soft smile on her face.

"Yes. Yes he was." Beatrix returned the smile, thankful.

As they made their way through the throng of people, her gaze settled on the duke who was gesturing wildly to Lady Southridge.

"Oh dear," Beatrix mumbled

"You have no idea…"

# CHAPTER TWELVE

"I DON'T KNOW HOW WE MISSED THIS," Curtis remarked with frustrated interest.

"To be honest, I wouldn't have thought of it if Beatrix—Miss Lamont hadn't pointed me in that direction."

"For it to be the duke? This entire time? It confounds me!" Curtis set aside the condemning parchment that was the key to the whole sordid mystery of Sir Kirby.

"But we have to act quickly, to strike while the iron is hot. He will not suspect that we have discovered his true identity... or intentions." Neville paced about the room.

"Indeed, but—" Curtis blew out a heavy sigh. "—I can hardly fathom it."

"I do believe that was the whole intention," Neville replied while shrugging into his great coat.

"One must admit that it is quite diabolical... brilliant even." Curtis carefully tucked the document into a leather folder.

"I'm not one to offer up compliments to criminals." Neville turned to face his friend, knowing his impatience leaked through to his terse tone.

"Right." Curtis cleared his throat, as if chastened, then stood.

"If you're quite finished complimenting the blackguard, shall we be away?" Neville gestured to the door with an unnecessary flourish of his hand.

Curtis simply shot him a dark look as he passed.

Neville kept his emotions under tight rein as he considered what lay before them. Kirby had done a remarkable job of cloaking himself as well as his intentions, which simply affirmed in Neville's gut that he was a desperate, dangerous foe.

"We'll take my curricle. It's still waiting outside from my arrival." Curtis hardly spared a glance behind as they strode to the door.

Once upon the conveyance, Curtis snapped the leather straps, and the matched greys jumped at his command, pulling them out from Mayfair District and toward the residence of Sir Kirby. The London air was thick with the scent of impending rain. "Of course it's going to downpour. We're in a curricle," Neville grumbled as he studied the heavy grey clouds.

"It will not," Curtis clipped, but his gaze darted upward.

Neville gave him a disbelieving glace but refrained from comment. The streets seemed overly full of horse and human traffic, causing their pace to slow. "This is taking too long," Curtis mumbled as he maneuvered around a recently spilled crate of potatoes.

"It's not far now," Neville replied, trying to keep sound reasoning. It would do no good to allow frustration to cloud his thoughts. No. He needed every wit about him.

"Thank the good Lord for Henry's directions. Look! There!" Curtis gestured to a hired hack who had just pulled up before the entrance to Sir Kirby's lodgings. Pulling the greys to the side, he watched as two men exited the conveyance and approached the door. Both men were well-dressed but carried leather folders, much like the one Curtis clung to.

"Barristers?" Curtis asked.

"I would appear so. If that is the case, then fortune is on our side, my friend."

"Indeed." Curtis glanced behind them then pulled the greys back onto the road. He paused them before Sir Kirby's door.

After exiting the curricle, Neville bounded up the stairs, Curtis at his heels. After sharing a glance, Neville placed a solid knock on the large black door.

"Yes?" A young butler answered the door, his expression faltering as he took in the two men before him.

"We are here to have an audience with Sir Kirby. We have information that concerns his current state of affairs." Curtis spoke with a professional tone.

Neville watched as indecision flickered across the face of the butler. "If you'll give me but a moment, my lords."

When the door closed, Neville spoke lowly, "Surely Kirby isn't as deep in the pocket as he'd like people to imagine if he cannot hire a proper butler. Surely, the man has little to no experience with the position."

"Indeed, he didn't even request our cards."

"Which is to our benefit."

"Exactly."

The door opened, revealing the butler once more. "Sir Kirby is currently not available, but he bids you leave your card—"

"It would be in your employer's best interest if he were to—"Curtis started.

"Bloody hell with it all." Neville shoved the butler aside and strode down the dimly lit hall.

"Gentlemen! I must insist! You cannot simply—" the butler tried but was silenced when Neville heard the sound of flesh meeting fist.

"I don't know if that was necessary, but I do approve of

the methodology." Neville glanced behind him as Curtis shook his hand once and jogged to catch up.

"Shut the door," Neville called.

A moment later, they paused before a closed door, muffling the voices within.

"Your case should be reviewed within the next week, sir—"

"That's too long! I don't have time for this!" Sir Kirby's voice rose.

"These things take time, sir. You must understand," another man spoke.

"So you've said! Far too many times for me to count!"

"This is a legal matter. Legal matters tend to require much patience as a thorough investigation must take place for something of this nature to even be considered altered in any way."

"I've given you every piece of documentation. It should be obvious to any fool who even glances at the case!"

"Have you heard enough?" Neville asked Curtis lowly.

"Indeed. Those gentlemen are the barristers conducting the case."

In the silence, they heard the men speak once more. "We'll take our leave now and will check with you in a few days' time."

Neville opened the door and strode in, glorifying in the horrified shock of Sir Kirby's face as he glanced from him to Curtis and back.

"Who the hell do you think you are?" Kirby stood, his face red with rage.

"That is a brilliant question," Curtis replied, a dry sarcasm lacing his tone.

"If that will be all, we will take our leave—" The two barristers stood, their expressions worried.

"No, I believe you'll wish to stay for this… introduction."

"Russell!" Kirby called, glancing behind the men.

"Your… capable butler is going to be nursing quite the

headache in a few hours...," Curtis replied with such a calm tone, it was chilling.

Neville circled the room, sizing up his opponent, waiting for the perfect moment to begin the destruction. "Do you know who I am?" Neville asked.

"No. And if I don't know you, then you must be nothing more than a common criminal," Kirby spat, glancing to the door as if evaluating his escape.

"That was unnecessary," Curtis replied, pretending offense.

"I know you!" One of the barristers took a step forward. "I never forget a face. And you — you're the one that solved that Prother case! I was on the floor when it was discussed. Neville, isn't it?" The man snapped his fingers, recognition lighting his expression.

"Ah, Prother... yes." Neville swallowed. Of course *that* would be the case discussed. Of course, the story that the man knew and what had actually happened were not one and the same.

Few circumstances surrounding those with wealth were.

"What has that to do with me?" Kirby growled, shooting a mutinous glance at the barrister.

"Ironically, the similarities are substantial... but unrelated," Curtis interjected.

"Kirby... now that you know who I am... shall I tell others who *you* are?"

"They all know who I am!" Kirby shouted, but it was clear that his confidence was faltering.

"Now... I'm not quite so certain of that," Curtis replied.

"Nor am I... especially after I discovered a very telling secret." Neville strode right up to Kirby, who stood shaking, his hands in fists at his side, eyes narrowed.

Leaning in, Neville whispered, "I've never been good at keeping these type of secrets."

"You have no proof." Kirby called his bluff.

"Ha!" Curtis's outburst interrupted the stare c between Neville and Kirby.

"I don't understand," the older barrister spoke.

"May I?" Curtis asked, and Neville nodded as he took a step back from Kirby, watching with satisfaction as the color drained from his face when Curtis withdrew the yellowed parchment.

"I have in my possession a verified copy of the marriage registry of St. George's from the year 1808, if you'll wish to authenticate." He went around to the barristers and displayed the document. "It states here that Sir Richard Kirby was, on the day of April 3, 1808, married to a woman by the name of Marianne Lamont Greene."

Neville watched as Kirby went absolutely still.

"And I have on the next page a document stating that Sir Kirby's wife met her end six months later."

"That proves nothing!" Kirby shouted.

"I'm failing to see the connection," the younger barrister questioned, his tone confused.

"We failed to see it at first as well," Neville answered, pacing before Kirby slowly, methodically, like water dripping — agitating and intending to drive one mad.

"It was never about the Lamont's fortune, was it?" Neville asked.

Kirby remained silent.

"It was about revenge," Neville spoke darkly. "A man with nothing to lose—"

"And everything to gain," Curtis finished.

"You can't prove that," Kirby threatened.

"So you think… but I don't have to. I simply have to say one name… to one person," Neville spoke smoothly, like silk over a dagger.

"He wouldn't even remember her name," Kirby spat.

"But you remember his."

Kirby hissed.

"Tell me, did she threaten to leave you the week after you were married, or did she wait a whole month?" Curtis asked condescendingly.

"A week? Perhaps he couldn't…"

"Silence!" Kirby shouted, his chest heaving, his body tense.

"Ah, I think we struck a nerve," Curtis spoke triumphantly.

"Do you think she even told him she was married? I'd have to say no… because she was already planning on leaving you."

"She loved me. It was he! He poisoned her mind against me! She — she—

"She wanted out. Away from you." Neville spoke the words with a deathly calm.

"He didn't even remember her! Didn't even attend her funeral when she died carrying his child!" Kirby yelled and, reaching swiftly, threw over a table. "He'll burn in hell for what he did to me — to her!" The crystal glass of brandy that had been sitting on the table flew toward the hearth and shattered against the stone, spraying the brandy into the flames, causing them to burst forth with a bright and hungry explosion of fire.

"And since you, a mere sir, cannot think to compete with a duke… you sought the more patient route. His wards," Neville completed.

"And with your dead wife's middle name Lamont… you were able to easily falsify what was necessary to avoid question."

"Knowing that even if it never happened, if you never got to his wards, eventually he'd have to face you."

"And then you'd have your final revenge."

"Did you really think you'd get away with murdering a duke?" Neville asked softly, ignoring the mutual gasp of the barristers.

"He would have known what it's like to suffer. His wife would have known *my* bloody pain," Kirby swore, his tone both angry and broken.

"Which is why you went to his residence every day at 4:00 p.m.

"The very time your wife died."

"He never even knew she was increasing," Kirby spoke with venom.

"That's because she wasn't," Neville replied, taking in the squint of Kirby as he me his gaze.

"If you would have read the report… she died of an opiate overdose… no evidence of her… increasing."

"She lied to you," Curtis finished.

"No, she… she—"

"Lied," Neville enunciated.

"Liar falls for liar. Romantic, is it not?" Curtis studied his nails and brushed lint from his jacket, as if they were merely discussing the weather.

Kirby's silence reigned in the room, acting as both his confession and his own awakening.

"In light of this new information…"The older barrister stood and cleared his throat. "…I do believe I need to summon a constable." He glanced to Neville then Curtis, and with their nod he left.

"She loved me…" Kirby's tone was broken.

"No, but I do believe that you loved her," Neville allowed.

"They'll hang me for sure," Kirby replied, his gaze frantically searching the room.

"You'll not escape." Neville took a menacing step forward.

Kirby lunged for the door, but Neville knocked him to the ground, giving him a right hook to the jaw. Kirby stilled, unconscious.

"Impressive." Curtis nodded his approval.

"I cannot tell you how long I've wished to do that." Neville stood and straightened his coat. "You, find me something to tie his hands," he called to the remaining barrister who stared at Kirby's body with wide-eyed shock.

"Y-yes, my lord."

Shortly after they tied Kirby's hands with some rope found in his desk, several constables arrived. Curtis quickly disclosed the proof and confession, with the barrister's confirming every detail.

As they carried Kirby's unconscious body out the door, Neville felt a heavy hand on his shoulder.

"Are you dealing well with this?"

"Yes," Neville replied, knowing what Curtis was asking. Because Kirby's story… could have been his. Even the similarity in the names was uncanny. But while Kirby plotted revenge, Neville was able to see the truth of the matter. Mary, his own betrothed, had sought pleasure elsewhere as well. When she'd discovered she carried a child, she'd tried to seduce him, but sensing something off, Neville had refrained from the temptation she'd presented. It was when he'd refused her that the truth had come out in a desperate flood. When he'd threatened to put her aside, she had left in a fury. A week later, she was found at his family's London residence at the bottom of the stairs. That was the Prother case… Mary Prother. The known story was that she fell down the slippery marble stairs. But the truth? Her suicide was her own revenge, attempting to frame Neville as the jealous lover. And it might have worked had her father's valet not killed himself the next day, a Romeo and Juliet act. A note was later found, confessing his love for Mary and their knowledge of her expecting, and something about not wanting to let a lie keep him from getting into heaven. Her parents, not wanting the world to know the shame, paid to keep certain information from the public's knowledge.

And, as such, lent to quite the amount of speculation concerning himself. Which was why he went into more of a reclusive state, and why he'd become involved with the war office.

And all such events led him to this moment.

To the beauty of finding love.

Beatrix.

"Are you with us, old man?" Curtis's voice called him back to the present, and he studied the scene before him. Two constables waited for his answer to some question.

"Pardon?"

"Is there anything you wish to add to Mr. Sheppard's statement?" one with a neatly trimmed mustache asked.

"No, no." Neville shook his head.

"Then I believe that's all we need. Er, what about the fellow out front knocked out?"

"He's the butler. I'm not sure what role he played."

"We'll take him in as well then, just to gather his statement. I think he's waking up."

The officers left, and Curtis rubbed his hands together. "I think our work here is done." He smiled.

"It would seem so. Shall we go to our next appointment?" Neville asked, his body tense with anticipation.

"I thought you'd never ask."

# CHAPTER THIRTEEN

"BEATRIX!" BETHANNY'S VOICE PULLED HER ATTENTION from the book before her as she retired in the library. As Beatrix glanced up, Bethanny scurried into the room and closed the door softly behind her, her brown eyes lit with excitement.

"He's here!" Bethanny clapped. She reached out, pulled her sister's hands, and helped her to stand. The book slumped to the ground, making a muted thud as Beatrix stood.

"Who?" Her heart wanted to believe it was Neville, but to do such would be quite the risk. And certainly her sister would not be so animated if the gentleman she'd referred to was Sir Kirby.

"Who?" Bethanny scoffed teasingly. "Neville...?" She let the word linger in the air, heavy with expectation.

"Neville?" Beatrix breathed, savoring the name and feeling a joy lighten her heart.

"Yes!" Bethanny took a step back and studied her sister. "This won't do." Immediately she stared tugging on Beatrix's hair, adjusting her dress, and picking at invisible lint on her skirt.

"How do you know?" Beatrix asked, tolerating her sister's

grooming.

"I… that is…" Bethanny blushed slightly. "Graham and I arrived at the same moment. Of course, my husband followed Neville and the duke into the study, all but slamming the door in my face," Bethanny grumbled.

"I highly doubt that." Beatrix giggled.

"I did try to stop the door with my foot, and I may or may not have listened at the threshold… but then the duke opened the door with me against it. I say, I already feel sympathy for his heir. The man has a wicked scowl." Bethanny shook her head.

"Wait… you were just arriving? You were supposed to be here hours ago." Beatrix glanced to her sister questioningly.

Bethanny's face bloomed with color. "We got distracted."

"I don't want to know any other details." Beatrix held up her hands, a wry grin teasing her lips.

"Nor will I offer any." Bethanny winked. "However, it is to your extreme benefit that we arrived when we did, because we now know of his arrival and have time to freshen up. I'm assuming he needs to inform the duke about Sir Kirby. You *did* hear of his arrest earlier today?" Bethanny paused, watching her sister's response.

"Yes! But I haven't heard any details. Did you hear anything of use while listening at the study door?"

"No." Bethanny pouted. "However, judging by the tone of the duke's voice, he was quite shocked, but I didn't hear anything more. Graham thinks the duke won't be entirely pleased with Neville once he sweeps you away." She winked.

"And you were surprised by that notion?" Beatrix rolled her eyes.

"No. I was simply providing my observation. I imagine the duke will be more amicable once Neville makes his intentions clear, and the duke has his feathers soothed with a formal request of his permission. Especially with this Kirby-mess all taken care of."

"It's now that I realized just why you were so worried about your relationship with Graham. The duke is quite... protective... is he not?" Beatrix shook off the thought of Sir Kirby, focusing on the delight of knowing Neville was there, speaking to the duke... of her. Wasn't he?

"Indeed..." Bethanny sighed, grinning slightly. "And Graham is the duke's close friend."

"Neville... is not."

"No, but I do not think that will impede his intentions." Bethanny smoothed her palm across Beatrix cheek.

"Am I presentable?" Beatrix stepped back and spun slowly.

"Stunning."

"I imagine they'll request our company soon," Bethanny assured.

"Not soon enough. I'm sure the duke will need to be informed quite thoroughly on the circumstances surrounding Kirby's arrest." Beatrix felt her heart pound with relief, yet acute anticipation. Was it truly all over? Had the nightmare ended?

A knock at the door caused Beatrix's heart to stutter then pound with fierce expectation.

"Yes?" Bethanny answered, moving to stand in front of Beatrix.

"Lady Graham, Miss Beatrix, your presence is requested in His Grace's study," Murray replied as he opened the library door with his usual unassuming manner.

"Of course, please tell His Grace we will be there directly."

Murray nodded and left.

Bethanny spun while reaching out and grasping her sister's hands. "Are you ready?"

"I was ready quite a while ago." Beatrix took a deep breath.

"Then let's not delay." Bethanny hitched a shoulder with a saucy wink.

Memories flooded her mind as she walked toward the study. How many times had she and her sisters slid down this very hall in their stockings, only to be scolded by Mrs. Pott, the housekeeper? How many times had she done the very same thing Bethanny had done earlier and pressed an ear against the duke's study door? Yet, it all seemed different, as if the atmosphere had changed, or maybe it was just her.

Bethanny paused just before the closed door and held up her hand for Murray to wait before opening it. Turning to her sister, she placed her hands on her shoulders. "Knowing the men within, they'll not discuss Kirby yet. Neville will wish to offer for your hand first, taking care of the most important. Therefore, take a breath… slow down your racing heart… because years from now, you'll want to remember these moments. I can't tell you how often I'll find myself remembering when Graham finally offered for me… when it was official, the faces of those present, the very scent of the air." She took a deep breath, as if remembering it again. "This is your moment. Own it, my love. Don't rush it, don't fight it… walk through it. Don't run." Bethanny pulled her into a hug.

"Murray?" Bethanny nodded to the door.

With a click of the knob, the door swung open silently, stilling all the murmuring conversation within the study. Beatrix noted how her sister walked through the door slowly, making a pointed entrance, shielding her sister's body with her own till she veered to the side to take her place beside her husband, Lord Graham.

Beatrix breathed in the room, committing the scent to memory, following her sister's advice and slowing down her heart's galloping cadence. As her eyes met Neville's, her heart stuttered to a stop then picked up its rhythm, not quickly, but steady, as if reassessing its steady beat to match another's. Then, because, well, this *was* her moment, she didn't pause but walked forward, purposefully, feeling her lips spread into a secret grin as Neville's gaze sharpened with understanding.

With a wicked grin, he wasted not one moment but started toward her as well, measured steps filled with purpose, with intention.

Only one word was spoken before his lips found hers.

"Finally."

It was the one word that summed up so much of what she needed to know.

*Finally*, the threat of Kirby was ended.

*Finally*, she was free to marry Neville.

*Finally,* she didn't have to worry about Berty's future because of Kirby.

*Finally*, she was free.

Warm lips captured hers, or maybe she started the kiss, but it mattered not. What mattered was that she was where she belonged.

In his arms.

Or was.

A heavy hand on her shoulder pulled her back from the delirious dream.

"Not in my study, not till you're officially married, and as God as my witness, never in front of me again," the duke's voice broke through, and she glanced away from Neville's smoldering gaze and the alluring temptation of his lips.

"Your Grace." Beatrix nodded to her guardian.

His face turned a frustrated shade of red, and as the world came back into focus, she was able to hear the stifled chuckle of Lord Graham and the not-so-hidden laughter from Bethanny and Carlotta.

"You laugh now. Just wait till you have an heir and must suffer the torment of their courtship." The duke glared at Graham.

"Lord willing, I'll only have sons."

"Which means you'll probably only have daughters," Lady Southridge chimed in.

Beatrix followed the voice, noticing the woman for the first time. Smiling at Lady Southridge, she bit back a laugh when the older woman winked.

"Now if you two will be so kind as to stand on opposite ends of the room?" the duke asked.

"You can't be serious," Bethanny spoke up.

"I am!"

"Oh for the love all of the—" Lady Southridge broke in.

"You saw them!" the duke interrupted.

"I'm not blind yet!" Lady Southridge shot back.

"Graham, if you don't cease your cackling," the duke threatened, turning to his friend, who held up his hands in surrender as he tried to control his amusement.

Beatrix glanced to Neville, shaking her head. "I do believe you'll fit in nicely," she spoke as she tilted her head slightly.

"Is that so?" He grinned approvingly.

"No more kissing." The duke pulled her back several paces.

Neville glanced heavenward as if petitioning for strength to keep from bursting into laughter.

Beatrix simply grinned, biting her lip as she gloried in the scene before her.

"Now…" The duke released her and moved into her line of sight, his bright blue eyes glancing between her and Neville, as if he didn't fully trust them.

Unable to resist the temptation, Beatrix made a slight movement, as if taking a step forward.

The duke froze and narrowed his eyes at her. "I wouldn't try that."

"Just checking," Beatrix replied teasingly.

The duke studied her for a moment. "Are you sure you wish to be forever matched to this?" The duke turned to Neville.

"To be fair, he hasn't actually asked yet," Bethanny chimed in before Neville could answer.

"Yes, I have," Neville answered, casting a secretive grin,

his eyes smoldering with their shared moment, stolen what seemed like so long ago.

"Pardon?" the duke interjected, his tone steely.

"In my defense, I did have Lady Southridge's approval."

The duke pinched the bridge of his nose. "Please tell me that I imagined that last statement. No. Dianna, tell me you didn't—"

"It was the only option after finding them—"

"What!" the duke roared then turned to charge toward Neville.

"Not like that! Control yourself, Charles!" Lady Southridge stood purposefully and placed her hands on hips, scolding the Duke of Clairmont.

The duke paused but didn't cease his glare aimed at Neville. "You could have clarified that in the beginning."

"Heaven's above." Lady Southridge glanced heavenward, shaking her head as if asking God why He'd seen fit to complicate her life with such people.

Beatrix bit back a bark of laughter. All she could think was how they could all say the same about her.

"You, sit." Lady Southridge pointed to the duke.

"And you… I've dealt with you far more than my share. There will be no more folly. Are we understood?" She then pointed to Neville, who nodded contritely.

When her gaze landed on Beatrix, Neville followed and winked at Beatrix.

Beatrix narrowed her eyes in response. "Beatrix! Your attention, if you please?" Lady Southridge spoke with an acute lack of patience.

"Yes?" Beatrix pulled her expression into one of polite detachment.

Lady Southridge shot her an unamused glare but seemed to decide against commenting on it. "Now… Lord Neville *does* need to ask Beatrix something quite important… regardless of if he's asked before or not. Now he has the blessing required, now it will count!" She nodded. "Now… the rest of us… out!" She made a shooing motion toward the door.

"I'll not leave them alone without a chaperone—"

"The door shall remain open," Lady Southridge answered.

"Pardon, but last I checked, this was *my* house and *my* ward!"

"And last *I* checked, five minutes alone would be quite acceptable. After all…" She turned to face Neville. "…five minutes is the perfect amount of time for a declaration, yet an unimpressive amount of time for anything… *else*… if you gather my meaning." Lady Southridge lowered her chin, waiting for Neville to respond.

He coughed slightly, as if covering a chuckle, but nodded his agreement.

"If I hear anything… rather, if I *stop* hearing conversation… I will not hesitate to make a very disruptive entrance." The duke pointed a finger between Beatrix and Neville, then seeming satisfied — or rather, overruled — he reached for Carlotta's hand and led her out of the room. Graham and Bethanny followed, Bethanny glancing behind her and giving a final, excited grin. Lady Southridge was last, and with a final wink, she all but closed the door, leaving only the smallest crack.

"I am constantly vacillating between anger and adoration toward that woman." Neville shook his head.

"She tends to have that effect on people," Beatrix answered, a rueful grin teasing her lips.

"Now…" Neville slowly approached her, as if savoring the moment. "…I was once told that there are some questions that must be asked… not simply told."

"I believe the word was *command*." Beatrix shot back, her tone amused.

"Close enough." He shrugged teasingly. "And since I seem to have not executed that perfectly in the past, I'm going to be sure I do it right this time." He reached out and grasped her hand. Tugging on the soft leather of her white kid glove, he methodically pulled on each finger till the garment was tossed to the ground. After removing his own glove, he laced his fingers with hers, intertwining not merely holding them. "I missed you like a sailor misses air when tossed into the sea," he murmured, his gaze searching hers.

A grin slipped across her lips unchecked. "I'm rather fond of you as well," she replied, but her tone was breathless as she studied the depth of his gaze, the determination in his expression, the possessive nature of his provocative grasp of her hand.

"And this is why I feel the need to simply tell you what to do. You take your freedom far too liberally." He raised a black brow. "However, I shouldn't wish to tame you." He tugged her hand till she took the short steps forward, and their toes touched. "No, I wouldn't want to tame you even the slightest…" he whispered against her lips before tasting them.

Lips, soft yet unyielding, captured hers, tugging and nipping, teasing them with the most delicious flavor of desire born of love. "And I would imagine you consider yourself quite uncivilized?" Beatrix whispered between kisses.

"Uncivilized? Of course I'm uncivilized… but who would wish to be tame? Not I, nor you. For therein lies what is full of abandon, what is full of adventure, of courage and curiosity. You, Beatrix, will never cease in provoking me…" He chuckled and kissed her hard, drawing out her lower lip. "…in the most delicious ways imaginable… but also outside of closed… or almost closed… doors. You make me think, evaluate life, consider other opinions because, in case you hadn't noticed, I rather think I'm correct most of the time."

"Which you are not," Beatrix added, a wry tone to her voice even as she lifted up on tiptoes to place another kiss to his warm lips.

"I am not always… but I am usually." Chuckling, he reached up and gently moved a curl away from her face then tucked it gently behind her ear. "I was right about you."

"Taking credit?"

"No, but I will be taking you… every last delicious inch of you… so if you'd please answer the question. I find I'm growing rather impatient." He growled as he kissed her once more, his hands pulling her in tightly, igniting a smoldering fire within.

"I'd answer if you'd simply ask." She pulled away just enough to speak before pressing a lingering kiss to his jaw, slightly prickly from his early shave.

"You're far too distracting for my good." He gently pushed her away. "Marry me," he whispered, searching her eyes, a wild gleam deep within his.

"I'd answer if you had *asked*…" Beatrix lifted an eyebrow, enjoying the moment, savoring it, committing every flash of his expression to memory.

He took a deep breath.

"Is it so hard to simply ask, Neville?" Lady Southridge's muffled voice came through the mostly shut door.

Beatrix bit back a bark of laughter at the shocked expression on Neville's face that transformed to irritated fury. With narrowed eyes toward the door, he spoke loudly, "Have you no self-respect?"

"No. And neither should you. Life's more fun that way. Also, you'll want to hurry it up. You've got less than thirty seconds before the duke barrels through this door. He has his pocket watch out…" She let the threat linger.

Neville glanced heavenward in much the same manner as the duke had when dealing with Lady Southridge.

"Beatrix—"

"On your knee, if you please," Beatrix cut in, grinning.

He lowered himself on to one knee and grasped her hand, his expression both amused and irritated. "Will you do me the profound honor of becoming my wife?"

"Yes," she responded immediately, her joy overflowing

into a wide grin that made her cheeks ache.

Neville wasted no time but stood and pulled her into a tight embrace before sealing her affirmation with a kiss.

The squeak of a door alerted them that their time had ended, and the heavy footsteps of the duke preceded his voice. "Release her," he barked, but with no bite in his tone.

"I'm assuming this means we have a wedding to plan?" Lord Graham's voice asked in a joyful manner.

"Yes," Lady Southridge answered.

Beatrix glanced to her, shaking her head.

"What?" The woman held her hand to her chest innocently.

"No one is fooled by your theatrics, Dianna," Graham replied.

"Here, here!" the duke answered.

"So when is the wedding?" Bethanny asked, rushing up to her sister and pulling her into a hug.

"Tomorrow."

The room went silent. Beatrix turned to Neville, her gaze meeting his then quickly darting about the room, taking in the shocked and unamused expressions of her family.

"Tomorrow happens to be my favorite day," Beatrix replied.

"Tomorrow?" the duke roared, striding toward Neville.

"Have you a special license?" Lord Graham asked once he found his voice.

"I secured one as soon as I returned to London." Neville nodded, his gaze darting to Lord Graham then resting on Beatrix.

"You could have told me that information earlier," the duke bit out.

"Have you considered… the implication of your hasty marriage?" Carlotta asked, her tone concerned.

"I have, but I will leave the final decision to Beatrix." Neville tilted his head slightly.

"I understand the implications, but, in truth, the *ton* will talk regardless." Beatrix hitched a shoulder.

"And I can set the record straight." Lady Southridge stood. "After all, Neville did court you while you were staying at Breckridge House… and the arrangements were already made before you came to London." Lady Southridge winked.

"Then it's decided." Beatrix nodded.

"But… don't you want a grand affair, Beatrix?" Bethanny came over to her sister and placed a gentle hand on her shoulder, studying her face.

"What I want… is him." Beatrix turned to Neville. "The sooner the better."

Neville's lips spread into a wide grin, his gaze dancing with delight and expectation.

"St. George's, tomorrow at noon. I am already on the docket." Neville brushed his coat slightly, almost nervously, as he cast a glance to the duke.

"By all means, make your plans without considering anyone else!" The duke glared.

"And what would have happened had I said no?" Beatrix placed her hands on her hips, shaking her head with amusement.

"I'd have reminded you that you are quite compro—"

Beatrix lunged forward and covered his mouth, glaring at him.

"What!" the duke roared.

"We already discussed this. It's like walking in circles with you two in the room!" Lady Southridge threw up her hands in exasperation. "Neville, you'll see your bride tomorrow at noon at St. George's. Till then, we have quite the amount of work to do, so if you'd please excuse us…" Lady Southridge grasped Beatrix's elbow softly, guiding her to the door.

"Please… wait." Neville's voice captured her attention, and she paused, curious at the almost pleading tone.

"I — that is — there is one more thing." Neville nodded,

walking toward her. "I love you," he whispered. Leaning forward, he pressed a tender kiss to her head. "I love you more than breath… and thank you that tomorrow you'll marry of all men… me." He murmured against her skin, his soft breath warm and inviting.

"I love you," she whispered back, eyes closed as she took in the heaven that was that moment.

"I should have said it earlier."

She glanced up and met his earnest gaze. "I know," she replied.

He grinned and took a step back, his expression both pleased and in wonderment.

"Perhaps it is a good thing you say vows tomorrow. I cannot imagine the hurdle of keeping you two apart for a long engagement," Lady Southridge remarked, her gaze warm.

"I'll drink to that, what say you, old man?" Graham turned to the duke, raising an eyebrow of inquiry.

"I believe I'll need more than one drink," the duke replied but without a bite, simply an accepting tone.

"You men drink your sorrows away. Ladies?" Lady Southridge called. The rustle of skirts accompanied Carlotta and Bethanny as they strode from the room with Beatrix and Lady Southridge.

"Beatrix? I'm sure you wish to know what happened with Sir Kirby?" Carlotta asked hesitantly.

"Yes…" Beatrix took a deep breath.

"If you wish, Neville or the duke will explain it tomorrow, but I rather thought you'd like to know now," Carlotta replied as they walked down the hallway.

"I would. I'm sure Neville will give me greater detail later, but I'd like to know the general idea." Beatrix considered Carlotta.

"Understandable." Carlotta nodded. "It is quite fantastical. You see, Kirby never was after you or your fortune," Carlotta explained.

"Pardon?" Beatrix turned swiftly to face Carlotta.

"It was about the duke… and revenge." Carlotta went on to explain the whole ordeal.

Yet, when she finished, as much as Beatrix was relieved to have everything over, she considered Carlotta. "And how are *you* dealing with such an accusation toward the duke? Obviously, it was before he knew you, but still…" Beatrix bit her lip then glanced to a wide-eyed Bethanny.

"As you said, it was far before our relationship and, as such, is the past. Girls, let me explain something." Carlotta took Beatrix's and Bethanny's hands, and Lady Southridge took a step back, watching with a warm maternal gaze. "Your husbands — or future husband—" She glanced to Beatrix. "—are human. As are you. Therefore, you'll all need forgiveness each day, and you'll need to accept it freely and give it freely. Sometimes choices from the past will affect your future. And you can grow angry, bitter and hateful, or you can use those circumstances to grow, to see where your husband, or you were… and how you've grown. I'm… I'm not who I once was. I'm braver, stronger, and smarter even. Why would I deny that same understanding of growth to my husband?" she asked.

Beatrix nodded, seeing her sister do the same from the corner of her eye.

"Now… since the past is behind us… let us look to an amazing future… starting with tomorrow, shall we?" Carlotta smoothed Beatrix's hair then squeezed her shoulder.

"And I have the best way to start," Bethanny chimed in. "Beatrix, come with me. I have the perfect gift for you." She tugged on her sister's hand and pulled them toward one of the vacant guest rooms.

"Now, if we make a few alterations, I do believe you'll have an ideal dress for your wedding tomorrow." Bethanny pushed open the door and strode to a large mahogany wardrobe. "I asked the duke to keep a few items from when I sorted through some of Mother's crates we still had stored."

She searched the clothing and found a muslin gown in a buttery yellow. A matching soft white silk shawl with embroidered flowers complimented it.

"It was Mother's wedding dress," Bethanny spoke reverently as she laid the dress upon the bed. "You're of a similar size, I'd imagine. Shall we see?" Bethanny turned to face her sister, her eyes moist with unshed tears.

"Mother's dress? You found it." Beatrix reached out and fingered the soft fabric. "Thank you," she whispered, her throat thick with emotion.

In short order, Beatrix careful donned the garment.

"I cannot fathom how it fits so perfectly," Lady Southridge spoke with awe.

"Indeed. I doubt it needs any altering at all!" Carlotta chimed in, walking around Beatrix.

Beatrix studied her reflection, a thousand emotions swirling within.

"It's perfect, Beatrix… perfect," Bethanny spoke with reverence.

"It is," Beatrix replied.

"In every way."

# CHAPTER FOURTEEN

NEVILLE RESISTED THE URGE TO PACE the front of St. George's as he awaited the moment when Beatrix would stride down the aisle and finally become his wife. He glanced to Curtis, who was standing up with him, his expression amused as he took in Neville's posture.

Narrowing his eyes, Neville glared at the man.

Unrepentant, Curtis bit back a chuckle.

"Someday…" Neville gestured slightly to his position, conveying that Curtis would someday be the one waiting.

Expecting a scoff or for Curtis to wave it off, Neville was shocked when Curtis's color heightened, as if blushing. His gaze darted away, as if trying to hide his reaction to Neville's implication.

The organ began playing, drawing his attention back to the present. Every other thought disappeared as movement captured his attention from the back of the sanctuary. The doors opened, and with a measured grace that simply stole his breath, Beatrix walked in. Her hair was softly pulled up with gentle curls highlighting her beautiful face. Her eyes, alive with anticipation, a secret delight, captivated and held him spellbound. She was glorious, beautiful, and breathtaking.

And in a few minutes… she'd be his.

Without delay, he grasped her hands, silently damning the gloves she wore, wishing for the warm touch of her skin.

Soon.

The priest cleared his throat and began the ceremony. Neville grinned as he watched Beatrix's gaze rest on him. Her golden brown eyes searched his, and he delighted the soft blush caused her cheeks to glow.

The priest cleared his throat.

Neville glanced to him.

"My lord?" The priest raised a white bushy eyebrow in expectation and a little impatience.

"Yes?" Neville asked, feeling slightly chagrined for not paying attention at his own wedding, but in his defense, his wife to be was alluringly distracting.

"I'll begin again." The priest sighed and recited the vows he expected Neville to have heard the first time.

Paying careful attention and ignoring the amused expression on Beatrix's beautiful face, he repeated after the priest, swearing that he'd adore his wife in sickness, in health, for wealth or for poverty… in all circumstances before God.

It was no small thing to pledge one's life, one's heart. And Neville wasn't simply repeating the words. They were his litany, his vow, as he lost himself in the warm gaze of the woman who had so utterly stolen his heart.

Beatrix solemnly promised the same vows, her gaze unflinching, warm and loving as she pledged her heart to him.

And, blessedly, the priest finished then announced the final words that Neville had waited so long to hear.

His *wife*.

And since she was finally, officially his, he didn't wait for the priest's invitation to kiss his bride.

Because when one is married, he may have kisses whenever he wishes, correct?

And he wanted to kiss his wife that very second, the moment it was official. Sealing it, possessing it, glorying in it.

So, before the priest could finish the declaration, he drew her in, sealing each promise he had made upon her lips.

Again…

And again.

Till the priest clapped the old book of common prayer shut. Loudly.

But even then, he simply withdrew far enough to gaze into her eyes, to read the love he could see she hid there for him.

Him alone.

"Impatient, aren't we?" she teased.

"For you? Always… now about the wedding breakfast. Must we—"

"Yes. And you'll enjoy every moment." Beatrix nudged him slightly, flirting.

"Not likely… but I'll pretend to," he baited, lacing his fingers through hers. "Which truly is further proof that for you, I'd do anything," he replied as he led them down the aisle.

"Because pretending to enjoy breakfast is harrowing," she flirted, poking him in the ribs.

"When I'd much rather be enjoying my wife, it's not just harrowing. I'll be doing the impossible." He tasted her kiss once more before helping her climb into the carriage that would convey them to the duke's residence for the intimate wedding breakfast.

"How long?" Neville asked his wife as he promptly picked her up and sat her on his lap.

Which was a brilliant and tortuous idea. So close yet so far away.

"At least a few hours." Beatrix hitched a shoulder as she raked her fingers through his hair.

Had she any idea how it drove him mad when she did such things? Already he was in no state for polite company, and she was only making it worse.

Or better, depending on one's perspective.

"You're a wicked minx."

"I do believe I'll pay for my many sins later," she whispered in his ear.

"Good Lord, woman, you can't say such things if you wish me to survive the wait." His heart quickened as she kissed his neck slowly, her warm mouth making his body catch fire.

"What things?" She feigned innocence as her hand tickled the outside of his leg.

The carriage halted, breaking the sensual haze surrounding him, blinding him to the knowledge that he was stuck in purgatory… heaven so close, yet not within reach.

Yet.

"You have ninety minutes," he ground out, "then you are mine. Over—" He tugged on her sleeve, exposing her shoulder. "—and over—" He nibbled on her warm flesh. "—and over again."

"What breakfast?" She sighed, leaning into him.

"Are you two quite done in there?" Lady Southridge called from outside the carriage. "Neville, she deserves more than to be seduced in the carriage!"

Neville shot a glare toward the carriage door. "Little does she know I'm the one being seduced." He shook his head.

"Over… and over… and over…" Beatrix teased, tugging on his hair once before standing and adjusting her dress from her exposed shoulder.

"You'll pay for that."

"I hope so." She winked and waited by the door, as if not understanding why he was still sitting down.

"Neville!"

Lady Southridge's voice had the effect of ice water, and he found he was ready to face his final torture far quicker than he had expected. As they ascended the stairs, Graham and the duke were waiting at the entrance, their faces far too amused for his intolerant attitude.

Beatrix blew him a kiss and headed toward her sister, Lady Graham.

"Welcome to hell." Graham slapped him on the back.

"Indeed." Neville didn't remove his gaze from his wife but studied every curve.

"Hell, but remember… heaven is only a few hours away." Graham goaded.

"Ninety minutes," Neville corrected, making eye contact with Graham.

"Ah…" He nodded in understanding, a grin bending his lips.

"You really are in hell then." The duke laughed, entirely too pleased with himself.

"Pardon?"

"Bethanny only made it thirty minutes." Graham raised an eyebrow of challenge, of conquest.

"Damn you," Neville growled.

"I had a little longer to wait." The duke shrugged. "But not much. I do believe I find this form of punishment better than anything I could have conjured up for your… premature assertion of Beatrix's affection." The duke nodded once.

Neville had nothing to say, nothing to add. Rather, he glared at the men before him and cast his longing gaze toward his wife.

Ninety minutes.

In hell.

He could survive.

Because bliss waited just on the other side.

Just then, Beatrix turned and winked a seductive little invitation.

On the other hand, ninety minutes could potentially kill him.

# CHAPTER FIFTEEN

BEATRIX TRIED TO HOLD IN HER amusement at her husband's extreme ill humor. She knew the depth of his frustration — she felt it as well — yet it was endlessly amusing to watch him pace like a caged tiger.

The breakfast began, and she pushed her food around the plate, her stomach tight with butterflies of anticipation. By the time an hour chimed on the clock, she was finished.

Surely they could escape early? How long had she waited to have him to herself, to finally be free of every hurdle between them? Now the final barrier was simply time.

Surely that could be flexible, could it not?

So, with simply a wink to Bethanny, Beatrix walked around the room and found her husband brooding in the corner with his eyes on the clock. He had surely been a good sport, but it was time.

Deftly, she slid her hand across the breadth of his shoulders then up his neck to his hair, knowing how even the slightest tug drove him mad.

"For an innocent, you're quite adept at torture." He turned to face her, his eyes smoldering with restraint.

"I was thinking… isn't it about time we amended that?" she asked, tugging on his hand and leading him toward the exit.

"Your ability to tempt or your innocence?" he asked, eyes blazing with anticipation.

"We'll see, won't we?"

Beatrix turned and darted toward the carriage, knowing she wasn't going to win an award for speed, but not caring. She stifled a squeal when her husband swung her into his arms and made haste toward the carriage. He gently eased her in and thumped the ceiling before he was even seated.

"It's your turn to burn," Neville whispered before pulling her onto his lap. He slowly reached his hand to her ankle and lifted her skirt slightly as his fingers gently traced the line from her ankle to her knee.

Her body reacted with heat swirling inside her belly, causing her heart to beat rapidly, her breath to come quicker, as if she were doing more than simply sitting, but running swiftly! His lips teased her own, his teeth gently biting her lower lip. The peppermint flavor of him imprinted itself on her memory. And, impossibly quick, the carriage stopped, presumably before Neville's residence.

Without a word, he lifted her off his lap and stood. He alighted from the carriage and, in a delft movement, lifted her into his arms and took the steps, two at a time. His butler was waiting by the door and swung it open, but he was nothing but a blur as Neville strode wordlessly past and toward the stairs. As he ascended, he called back, "See that we are not disturbed."

To which the butler simply replied, "Of course, my lord."

The butler's voice was abruptly cut off by the distinct sound of Neville's arrival on the top stair. A few steps later, Beatrix bit her lip when her husband's embrace tightened as he leaned forward and twisted a knob.

After he kicked the door open, the room came into view, a

rich and wide space with dark woods and a distinctive scent that was clove and peppermint, the very scent she associated with Neville. Lowering her to the ground, his hands lingered on her waist, tracing her shape. His hands were warm, yet she felt her body erupt in goose bumps with heady anticipation. His eyes burned with smoldering desire as he stepped back and kicked the door shut with his boot.

"Are you going to lock it?" Beatrix asked, glancing from the door to her husband, slightly shy, yet unwilling to let it compromise her bold desire.

"Are you planning on leaving?" Neville asked, taking a slow step toward her, daring, captivating, and weaving a spell around her with the wicked intent in his gaze.

Wordlessly, Beatrix shook her head.

She watched as her husband tugged off his gloves then tossed them to the side.

"I've always hated gloves… especially on you." He reached down and pulled her hand up, caressing her wrist before unfastening the pearl button and tugging each gloved fingertip till the silken accessory slipped to the ground. He repeated the same with her other hand. Palms together, he lifted their hands up and laced his fingers between hers. His grip was warm, comforting, yet anything but tame.

"I've waited for what seems like forever, and now that I have this long-awaited moment… I want time to stand still," he confessed, releasing one hand and cupping her cheek, warming her face.

His dark locks tempted her, and, without hesitation, she gave into the siren call of his soft hair. That was the beauty of the moment, that every temptation was simply an invitation. Weaving her fingers through his thick mane, she grinned when his eyes closed, and he leaned into her touch. It was humbling, yet empowering, to have such control, such power over another. But such was the nature of love, to completely give oneself over to the other, for better or worse. She'd not take such a gift lightly.

But tonight… tonight was a celebration. The final declaration, the physical completion of everything already in her heart, in his heart. And she was through with waiting.

As if reading her thoughts, Neville's eyes opened, spearing through her with their heat. Wordlessly, he placed a warm kiss to her neck, swirling his tongue along her flesh, igniting it. Warm hands reached around and began to unfasten the blessedly few buttons along her back. When finished, he slid the dress off one shoulder. He leaned down and lavishly kissed it, marking it as his own. Turning his attention to the other shoulder, he removed the dress from it as well and showered kisses along the tender flesh that seemed to burn at his touch. The dress pooled at her feet, forgotten, as he turned his attention to the laces at her back, loosening the stays.

Swallowing, Beatrix pulled in a deep breath, trying to control her body's powerful reaction to her husband's ardent attention. Forcing her eyes into focus, she reached up and tugged at his cravat, loosening the silk then tossing it aside, letting it float to the ground, no longer necessary. With the garment removed, she could see the movement of his throat, his Adam's apple moved slightly, and she glanced up to meet his gaze.

"So beautiful," he whispered reverently, "and still so very clothed." He grinned slightly and turned her so that her back faced him. In short order, the final stays were loosened, and the corset slid to the ground.

'"My lady." He grasped her hand, lifted it, and twirled her so that she'd once again face him. His gaze grew fiercely possessive as he took in her state of undress. Gently, he assisted her to step over her removed garment.

"Why thank you… but I must say… this is disappointing." Beatrix took a step back, growing more comfortable, even in the small, chemise underpinnings she wore.

"Disappointing?" Neville's brow furrowed, even as his

gaze greedily took her in.

"Indeed. Am I not allowed the same benefits that you enjoy?" Beatrix inquired, stepping forward and running a finger along his chest and under his coat. "Honestly… still in your coat? For shame," she teased and tugged at the black lapel.

"A thousand apologies," he replied and shrugged out of the finely cut garment. "What else would the lady request?" He held his arms out, his gaze inviting.

Beatrix walked around him. "Your shirt, sir. It offends me."

"I'll burn it." He removed it quickly, bursting the buttons and sending them scattering along the wood floor.

"But my view is still inhibited… and that will not do." Beatrix paused before him, tapping her chin as she pressed her other hand against his undergarment.

"We cannot have that," he crooned. In one swift movement, he crossed his arms and pulled the tighter shirt over his head and tossed it aside. His stomach was a delicious mix of hills and valleys that cut down to where his breeches remained. Her gaze lingered on his chest, a solid and powerful display of what she already had felt under his shirt before.

"Impressive." She bit her lip as her gaze met his, a flash of heat jolting through her at the pleasure in his gaze.

"I'm entirely pleased you approve." He took a step forward, his shoulders flexing, his body radiating an inviting warmth she wanted to melt into. "However, I do believe we're about even." He traced the fine strap of her chemise. "While a fine garment, it is most assuredly useless." He leaned forward and tugged on the shoulder strap with his teeth playfully.

"Say the word," Beatrix teased breathlessly, feeling his warmth call to her.

"Please." The word was a hot whisper against her shoulder.

Turning, Beatrix removed the chemise and, not wanting to

prolong it further, removed her other underpinnings. Feeling wicked, she simply cast a gaze over her shoulder. Her body bloomed with heat at the hungry gaze of her husband.

"So that is how we're playing, is it?" he asked, his voice thick with desire.

Rather than giving her his back, as she'd assumed he would, he strode forward and leaned his warm flesh against hers. She could feel his hands tugging at his breeches and heard the sound of them hitting the floor several feet way after he tossed them.

Just as she was about to speak, a warm tongue traced her back, licking the flesh as her husband stood behind her. His heated flesh met hers, consuming her, setting her on fire with a smoldering desire that only grew with every passing moment. His mouth was hot at her neck, tasting, teasing, provoking the most delicious desire from within her.

After spinning her to face him, his mouth captured hers, ravaging it, claiming it. Strong arms banded around her, pulling her in tightly. Hands roamed her curves, as if memorizing, exploring, devouring.

"I love you. Every inch, every flavor, every breath," he whispered. "Say my name," he demanded as he pressed into her, guiding her toward the bed behind them.

"Edmond."

"Louder."

"Edmond!" she all but cried, loving the word, owning its power over her, the truth of the familiarity of it all.

He kissed her deeply, possessively, slowly breaking the seal of their lips. He picked her up then gently laid her on the bed. A shiver broke out across her flesh, as if an immediate reaction to missing her mate, her love, her husband.

"Beatrix." He whispered her name as he studied her, his expression reverent.

She took the moment to study him, delighting in every aspect of his glory. A moment later, her husband knelt on the bed, the soft mattress dipping under his welcomed weight.

No longer chilled, Beatrix lost herself in the warmth of her husband's skin as it covered hers, completing every intention in their hearts.

# CHAPTER SIXTEEN

NEVILLE STUDIED HIS WIFE AS SHE sipped her tea while propped up in their bed.

*Their* bed.

Truly, he didn't think he could adore her more than when she'd agreed to marry him, yet when she'd walked down the aisle at St. George's, it was as if that love had doubled. Then, last night after she'd turned into the most playful lover imaginable, he woke up feeling as if his heart had grown several sizes. She was a wonder, his own miracle, and he'd not miss one moment glorying in the beauty of that rare find.

"Miss me already?" his wife asked with a secretive grin she tried to hide behind her teacup.

"I do believe the question is if you miss me," he countered, tugging on the sheets as she had them hiding the glory of her naked body.

Good Lord, the woman had the body of a goddess. Oh, he had imagined, but last night, he'd explored every blessed inch. And as soon as he was assured she was properly fed and hydrated, he was going to do the same.

Over and over.

As promised.

She tugged on the sheet, hiking it higher.

He pulled it, trying to snatch it from her grip.

She shook her head, her luscious brown locks dusting her shoulders with the movement. Surely, in all heaven and earth, there was not a more beautiful sight.

"Edmond," She scolded playfully.

How he loved hearing his name on her lips.

Although, his favorite was when she—

"What are you thinking? You have a particularly wicked grin on your face." She tilted her head slightly, studying him.

"About you," he answered, secretively wrapping the sheet around his hand and waiting.

"Oh?" she asked.

"Indeed. I was simply thinking about how much I love hearing you say my name."

"Your name? Like this… Edmond?" She grinned then took a sip of her tea.

The damn liquid had to be cold by now.

"Yes, but I wasn't referring to that particular circumstance." He chuckled as her face heated with a blush.

"Come love, there's no need to be shy." He used her momentary fluster to tug the sheets and succeeded in removing them from her inexcusable modesty.

She gasped and covered herself with her hands.

"Do not block such a lovely view— Wait!" He glanced to the discarded teacup. "How long has it been empty?" he asked, eyes narrowing as his wife giggled.

"Whatever do you mean?" She lost the fight and laughed deeply, the delicious sound filling the room and igniting his burning desire once more.

"Minx." He shook his head, and reached over and pulled her into the lee of his body. "You're chilled," he remarked as he traced kisses down her shoulder toward the particularly delicious landscape before him.

"Wait—" she gasped then pulled back slightly so that she could meet his gaze.

"Carlotta… she told me everything… about Kirby."

"I truly do not wish to speak of that blackguard right now," Neville replied, his tone impatient.

"I understand… but—"

"But I haven't spoken with you about it… and fault is mine. What do you wish to know?" He bit his cheek and tasted blood, hating even the thought of the man who had tried to separate him from the beautiful woman so gloriously naked beside him.

"I simply want to know one thing."

"Blessed providence," he whispered reverently.

She raised a wry brow.

"Apologies." He cleared his throat and glanced away, gathering his control.

"There's no way he could go after Berty?" she asked, her tone small.

Every protective instinct overwhelmed every other sense. Pulling her in tightly, he kissed the top of her head. "No. It's finished. It's done." He held her a moment till he sensed her body relaxing.

"Thank you. I don't think I've even said that yet." Her tone was relieved, yet grateful.

"Anything less wouldn't have been love, my sweet wife." She leaned back and lifted her gaze to meet his. "Love fights when there is a battle. It seeks till it finds, it searches till it's found, it doesn't rest, doesn't give up, doesn't seek itself, but the blessing of the other. It stands for what is right, what is true, what is lovely and beautiful. It's the one reliable truth in a world that compromises on so many other things. It's patient." He offered with a grin as he leaned down and placed a chaste kiss to his wife's lips.

"Exceedingly patient," she whispered against his lips, "even when it doesn't need to be." She invited and deepened the kiss as her arms wound around him, pulling him in tightly.

Not needing further encouragement, he vowed with his body the truth he had spoken.

# EPILOGUE

*Seven years later*

"TRULY, YOU ARE A VISION. I honestly questioned if I'd ever see this day." Beatrix, Countess of Neville, tilted her head in a decidedly motherly fashion as she studied her youngest sister, Roberta Lamont.

"I hesitate to ask why," Berty replied, studying her very wide sister. Truly, there was no other way to describe her sister. While there was much debate on the matter, it was her personal opinion that the Neville brood was about to grow by two. Surely the woman had to be carrying twins to be that large!

"If you make any further comment on my size, I'll… sit on you," Beatrix replied, her eyes narrowing.

"I was thinking nothing of the sort."

"You're a lousy liar."

"Are we all set?" Lord Neville strode into the drawing room, his gaze intent on his wife.

He was famous for that gaze. Truly, from the first ball where they'd attended as husband and wife, the gossip had spread like wildfire, but not as one would assume. They were that season's idyllic love match.

It was sickening, yet sweet at the same time.

As she grew into her majority, she found that she rather wished a gentleman would look at her the same way.

Like she hung the sun, moon, and stars.

"Beatrix, love, you need to be off your feet." Neville guided his wife over to a chair and set her feet upon a stool. Leaning in, he kissed her, and Berty averted her eyes, knowing it was likely not going to be a chaste kiss.

Seriously, it was no wonder they had five children already. Of course, that Beatrix had produced one set of twin girls had added to their heirs considerably.

Neville all but strutted about when one mentioned his brood.

Of course, Beatrix was no less proud. Just, she was so wide she couldn't strut but waddle—

"Truly, I know what you're thinking," her sister cut in again.

"Is it a mother thing? Do you gain this ability to read minds once you give birth? Inquiring minds wish to know!" Berty grumbled.

"Yes," Neville and Beatrix answered together then chuckled.

"Where is Bethanny?" Berty lamented.

"Well…" Beatrix glanced away as did Neville.

"Why Berty! You're simply stunning! I never thought I'd see the day." Lady Southridge strode into the room, still spry at her age.

"You and everyone else apparently," Berty shot back, narrowing her eyes at her sister. "And where did you say Bethanny was? She promised she'd be here! It's my debut. She *has* to be here," Berty whined, unable to restrain herself.

"Bethanny? Oh, I thought you knew, Berty," Carlotta remarked as she entered the now-crowded room.

"Knew about what?" Berty ground out. For as many

people as were talking, there was precious little actually being said.

"She's… well, we think she's expecting." Carlotta clapped her hands.

"Again?" Berty blinked.

"This is only number three," Beatrix interjected.

"But, but…" Berty felt her shoulder slump. "She's sick, isn't she?" she asked, already knowing the answer.

"Yes, but Graham sent a missive this morning saying she was going to try and make it tonight." Carlotta nodded then strode up to Berty and adjusted her gown. "You're going to be a wild success tonight, love. The duke and I, we are so proud of you." She placed a loving hand on Berty's cheek. "Truly, to have your debut, it's quite a spectacular night. One we've both waited for — and dreaded — knowing that we'd have to bless the intention of some young man seeking your heart." Carlotta's lip trembled slightly. "And to see you in such a beautiful dress…" She shook her head, tears welling up.

Was it truly *that* astounding for her to be wearing a dress? She was a young lady! What did they expect? Her to show up in a tiger costume?

"All is ready," Murray announced, "and Lady Graham is on her way." He winked at Berty.

"Thank heavens." Berty breathed, thankful that her oldest sister, the one so much like their mother, was going to be present on this, the most important night of her life.

As she walked down the hall toward the ballroom, the stars in the night sky twinkled, the moon glowed. It was truly stunning.

On a night like tonight, anything could happen.

Even love.

# ABOUT THE AUTHOR

KRISTIN VAYDEN'S inspiration for the romance she writes comes from her tall, dark and handsome husband with killer blue eyes. With five children to chase, she is never at a loss for someone to kiss, something to cook or some mess to clean but she loves every moment of it! She loves to make soap, sauerkraut, sourdough bread and gluten free muffins. Life is full of blessings and she praises God for the blessed and abundant life He's given her.

# ACKNOWLEDGEMENTS

THANK YOU TO EVERY READER who has read this series! Without you, this book wouldn't have ever had a chance to tell the amazing story of Lord Neville and Beatrix. Thank you for every note you've written, every post, every giggle over Lady Southridge's antics, and every bit of love you've shared with me. You guys are the best in the world, and I'm thankful for each one of you!

# OTHER BLUE TULIP BOOKS

BY MEGAN BAILEY
*There Are No Vampires in this Book*

BY J.M. CHALKER
*Bound*

BY ELISE FABER
*Phoenix Rising*
*Dark Phoenix*
*From Ashes*

BY JENNIFER RAE GRAVELY
*Drown*
*Rivers*

BY E.L. IRWIN
*Out of the Blue*

BY J.F. JENKINS
*The Dark Hour*

BY KELLY MARTIN
*Betraying Ever After*
*The Beast of Ravenston*

BY NADINE MILLARD
*An Unlikely Duchess*
*Seeking Scandal*
*The Mysterious Miss Channing*

BY LINDA OAKS
*Chasing Rainbows*

BY C.C. RAVANERA

*Dreamweavers*

BY ANGELA SCHROEDER

*The Second Life of Magnolia Mae*

*Jade*

BY K.S. SMITH & MEGAN C. SMITH

*Hourglass*

*Hourglass Squared*

*Hourglass Cubed*

BY MEGAN C. SMITH

*Expired Regrets*

*Secret Regrets*

BY RACHEL VAN DYKEN

*Upon a Midnight Dream*

*Whispered Music*

*The Wolf's Pursuit*

*When Ash Falls*

*The Ugly Duckling Debutante*

*The Seduction of Sebastian St. James*

*An Unlikely Alliance*

*The Redemption of Lord Rawlings*

*The Devil Duke Takes a Bride*

*Savage Winter*

*Every Girl Does It*

*Divine Uprising*

BY KRISTIN VAYDEN

*To Refuse a Rake*

*Surviving Scotland*

*Living London*

*Redeeming the Deception of Grace*

*Knight of the Highlander*
*The Only Reason for the London Season*
*What the Duke Wants*
*To Tempt an Earl*
*The Forsaken Love of a Lord*
*A Tempting Ruin*

BY JOE WALKER
*Blood Bonds*

BY KELLIE WALLACE
*Her Sweetest Downfall*

BY C. MERCEDES WILSON
*Hawthorne Cole*

BY K.D. WOOD
*Unwilling*
*Unloved*

BOX SET — MULTIPLE AUTHORS
*Forbidden*

www.bluetulippublishing.com

CPSIA information can be obtained
at www.ICGtesting.com
Printed in the USA
LVHW090721260222
712087LV00020B/471

9 781515 244875